ONCE UPON A HIGHLAND LEGEND

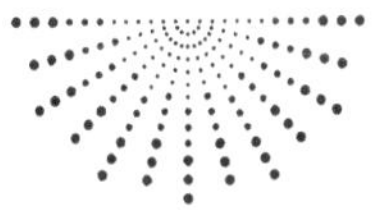

TANYA ANNE CROSBY

2nd Edition, July 21, 2014

This novella was previously published in the anthology The Winter Stone, April 21, 2014

Published by Oliver-Heber Books, LLC

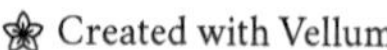

To all who still believe in faerie tales.

PRAISE

"Crosby's characters keep readers engaged..."

— PUBLISHERS WEEKLY

"Crosby sets out to show us a good time and accomplishes that with humor, a fast paced story and just the right amount of romance."

— THE OAKLAND PRESS

"Romance filled with charm, passion and intrigue..."

— AFFAIRE DE COEUR

"Crosby mixes just the right amount of humor... Fantastic, tantalizing!"

— RENDEZVOUS

"Crosby pens a tale that touches your soul and lives forever in your heart."

— SHERRILYN KENYON #1 NYT BESTSELLING AUTHOR

"My Queen of historical fiction for over two decades and she still leaves me breathless and wanting more!"

— BARB MASSABROOK, READER SINCE 1992

"Tanya Anne Crosby is a master of her genre ..." Laurin Wittig, Bestselling Author

"Love, honor, suspense, passion... all the good things we love in a Highlander Romance."

— SUZAN TISDALE, BESTSELLING AUTHOR OF ROWAN'S LADY

"Enchanting landscapes, breathtaking betrayal, and heartwarming passion herald Tanya Anne Crosby's triumphant return to ancient Scotland."

— GLYNNIS CAMPBELL, BESTSELLING AUTHOR

GUARDIANS OF THE STONE

SERIES BIBLIOGRAPHY

Highland Fire

Highland Steel

Highland Storm

Maiden from the Mist

Once Upon a Highland Legend

ALSO CONNECTED…

THE HIGHLAND BRIDES

The MacKinnon's Bride

Lyon's Gift

On Bended Knee

Lion Heart

Highland Song

MacKinnon's Hope

&

Angel Of Fire

MEDIEVAL SCOTLAND

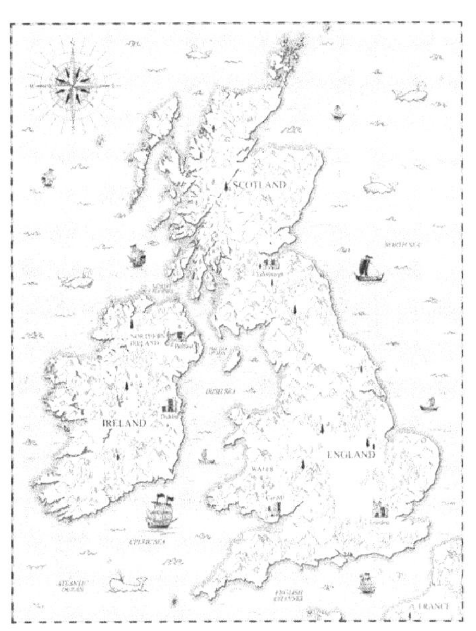

THE LEGEND OF THE WINTER STONE

Once upon a time, in a place time forgot, the last Pict King was betrayed by one he loved. Mourning his ignoble death, the Mother of Winter wept with grief, her icy tears shattering as they fell to earth. One did not. This pale stone she gave to the Guardians of the Old Ways, so that by its light all truths might be known. This is the tale of the Winter Stone...

CHAPTER ONE

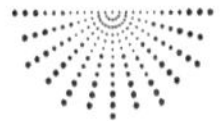

KINGUSSIE SCOTLAND, PRESENT DAY

"Are ye in Kingussie for the festival, lass?" the shopkeeper asked.

Blinking, Annie Ross peered up from the crystal she held in her hand, momentarily disoriented. It took her a muddled instant to recall exactly where she was—in a curio shop on High Street, waiting for her cousin to arrive. It wasn't like her to be so spacey. "No, actually… heading up to Devil's Point."

The old woman gave her a bit of a smirk but didn't comment; still Annie sensed she was amused by the choice of phrasing.

Okay, so she was actually headed to *Bod an Deamhain*. She and Queen Victoria's consort had something in common. Even in this twenty-first century, Annie had copped out, using the more modest name for a nearby mountain peak. The literal translation for anyone who knew better, was the "demon's penis." Apparently, despite the fact that vaginas now had plays named after them, Annie still couldn't say the word penis to strangers. But how ridiculous was that? She was a scientist after all. She blamed her pang of modesty on the skirt she was wearing. Somehow, it seemed entirely inappropriate to utter the word penis while wearing a short, plaid schoolgirl-type skirt that might have been better suited to a fetish poster than a Catholic schoolgirl.

As though to affirm her thoughts, the shopkeeper's gaze swept down to the hem of Annie's borrowed skirt. "American, are ye?" she asked, lifting the brow of her one good eye. The other had a patch over it.

Annie frowned. For some reason, the question left her feeling a bit defensive. As though only an American could wear such a getup, right? Well, her cousin—the previous and current owner of the skirt—was Scots to the bone, thank you very much.

Annie heaved a sigh. Unfortunately, her bags had been lost on the way to Kingussie and she'd had to borrow a clean shirt and a skirt from her cousin Kate, who didn't appear to own anything longer than six inches. For that matter, Kate's blouses didn't seem to have enough buttons either, and Annie had had to use a safety pin to keep her breasts from public display—not that her skirt length was any of the shopkeeper's concern, however.

Thankfully, Annie didn't much care about clothes one way or another. If it covered her bits, and kept her from getting arrested for indecent exposure, if it didn't smell like the boozer sitting next to her on the plane, well then she didn't care what she wore. Her own wardrobe was quite practical, and her long black hair usually found its way into a careless ponytail—the horsetail, her ex used to call it. That was why he was her ex—and *not* as Kate liked to put it, that Annie had commitment phobia. She was hardly afraid of men; she just had no patience for one-way relationships.

"My family's from here," she offered as she studied

the crystal in her hand.

"Aye? Whereabouts?" the shopkeeper asked. "Ye dinna sound much like a Scot. I do hope ye've brought something warmer for the climb, lass," she said, chattering on. "The wind'll freeze your paps."

Annie wasn't entirely certain what paps were, nor was she inclined to ask, but she lifted the arm her sweater was draped over, hoping it would be enough to convince the old woman to put away her maternal genes.

"Humph!" the shopkeeper declared. "Ye'll catch your death w' that! Ye'll need something warmer, dearie. We've tartans for sale," she suggested. "Certainly, one of the lot will match you're wee skirt."

Nice sales pitch, lady, but no thanks, Annie thought. "Thanks," she said, and went back to inspecting the crystal.

Bod an Deamhain was probably an eight-hour climb, but Annie didn't intend to go all the way up today. Only as far as she needed to go in order to survey the surrounding area. But she didn't volunteer that information because it wasn't anybody's business. She'd had enough of people trying to talk her out of it, including her cousin. "I'll be fine," she reassured.

"I'm sure ye will be," the old woman replied, and fell silent—finally—while Annie went back to examining the strange rock in her hand.

Unlike the rest of the crystals in the basket on the display case, this one was perfectly and unnaturally round, as though it had been created from a mold of some type. But it was heavy—not plastic. Testing its weight in the palm of her hand, she examined the striations at its center—milky ribbons. The first time Annie had peered into it, it had seemed colorless, though now it seemed to be turning a slight green…changing colors…like a mood stone. She glanced up to see that the shopkeeper was watching. The woman's one good eye flicked back and forth from the crystal in her hand to Annie's face…as though waiting for some reaction.

"Pretty," Annie remarked.

The shopkeeper nodded agreement.

Minerals weren't precisely Annie's forte, but she did like them, and in a way, it was how she had begun her career. As a child, she had completely annoyed her parents by collecting every ugly rock she had encountered. A visit to Mammoth Caves had been her childhood version of Disney World. And in a way, it still was, though as far as careers went she had taken an entirely different path. Archeology and Linguistic Anthropology were the cornerstones of her studies. Currently —as always—she was obsessing over the origins of *Lia Fàil*, otherwise known as the Stone of Destiny. It was the subject of her senior dissertation, but while it had netted her a passing grade for the thoroughness of her research, her professor had deemed it completely unoriginal and took off points.

Apparently—according to Professor Van Know-it-All—everyone was obsessed with the stone. Except that Annie wasn't simply obsessed, she was consumed. Her father had been too. She came by her obsessions honestly, and perhaps after all these years, she was simply trying to find a connection to her parents. She missed them both terribly and somehow it seemed that visiting the past through its artifacts blurred the lines between life and death…maybe a little.

As for the Stone of Destiny, she wanted to prove once and for all that the stone now on display in Edinburgh Castle wasn't the original—a gut feeling that just wouldn't die. But to do so she had to find some sort of physical evidence. Unfortunately, the currently acceptable theories had all found dead ends…except for one. For years Annie had been drawn to a particularly obscure report of a sighting near Kingussie, which also happened to be her father's birthplace—a happy coincidence, because Annie had been making yearly treks here since her childhood and she knew the area very well.

It made sense to her that the stone was hidden somewhere. Truly, if you were the abbot of Scone and the enemy was at your border, and you had three months to prepare for his arrival, knowing full well that he intended to steal Scotland's most valued symbol of freedom, would you simply leave it in plain sight? Not to Annie's way of thought. Who would do nothing and simply wait until Edward arrived? Not Annie. She would have hidden the stone somewhere in the hillside. And, in fact, the sandstone in the stone on display in Edinburgh had been quarried somewhere near Scone, while the original was supposed to have Biblical roots and had been hauled all the way from Ireland—supposedly. If that were true it would have been made of something entirely different. In general, there were just too many stories surrounding the stone, hinting at its inauthenticity, for there not to be some shred of truth in the legends...somewhere.

She kept hearing her dad whisper in her ear: *"Where there's smoke there's fire, Anniepie."*

"Amen," she muttered.

"What's that, lass?"

"Where did you get this?" she asked the old woman, holding up the stone now, curious over its makeup.

The shopkeeper's green eye sparkled. "Well, as legend would have it, these are the crystalized tears of Cailleach Bheur." She waved a hand over the basket.

"Cailleach Bheur?"

"Aye, she was—is—the Mother of Winter, guardian of all the Highlands," she explained. "These tears were born of her heartbreak, and she gave one to the keepers of the Old Ways, so that by its light all truths might be known."

"Interesting," Annie said. She hadn't heard that one before. Was she supposed to believe someone cried perfectly round tears the size of a golf ball?

The old shopkeeper was still watching her, and she would have walked away to avoid further conversation but the crystal held her transfixed. The others in the basket looked nothing like this one. She turned it in her hand, fascinated by its strange properties. It seemed to glow…as though it had its own energy source, but Annie couldn't see any seams in the crystal that might indicate it could be opened and a battery inserted—or even that one might have been placed inside and then sealed. Tapping the crystal carefully on the display case, she wondered if it was plastic. It looked and felt like solid quartz.

"Careful w' that," the old woman cautioned, her voice sounding as old as time itself. "It's *precious*."

Precious.

Annie smirked, flashing on Tolkien's ring, described exactly that way by those obsessed with it. But this was just a rock, she reasoned, and she wasn't obsessing over it. In fact, she already had enough obsessions. She didn't need another. She set the crystal down gingerly into the basket and walked away to examine a display of pamphlets, wishing her cousin would hurry. Late Kate, they called her. She peered up at the clock on the wall: 10:17. Late again—as usual—which certainly had been a good thing yesterday while Annie had had to stick around the airport to fill out missing-bag reports. But this morning, it was simply annoying, because Annie couldn't wait to get up into those hills.

Down the street she could hear the sounds of festivity beginning as people congregated for the coming parade. She wanted to get out of here before then. Apparently, there was a heritage festival going on to celebrate the town's historic presence. Annie thought maybe Kingussie had been established sometime during the Eighteenth Century, and a glance at a pamphlet verified the fact. Before then, it had been nothing but pinewoods. Originally called *Ceann a' Ghiùthsaich,* Kingussie was Gaelic for "head of the Pine Forest"—the forest being the vast Caledonian pinewoods that had once witnessed King Arthur's battles and the demise of the Picts—incredibly romantic histories that had been at the center of a million bedtime stories all shared by Annie's father. The ancient woods, formed after the last ice age, were nearly vanished now. Annie read somewhere that they were down to something like thirty-eight sites, all spattered across the Highlands. The land surrounding *Bod an Deamhain* was nearly devoid of trees now, though Annie would have loved to see it the way it had appeared a thousand years ago.

She stared hard at the crystal, wishing with all her heart that she might have seen it for herself, and realized suddenly that she had unconsciously returned to the basket and had retrieved the crystal. This time while she held it she thought she detected threads of pink.

It *was* changing colors.

Mood stones were made of thermo tropic liquid crystals that responded to changes in temperature, altering the molecular structure so that light reflected through it as various colors—a bit like a prism. But this wasn't exactly like a mood stone. The colored striations were too deep to be reacting to her body temperature, and the colors were vague, almost like an aura. She had never in her life encountered such a curious mineral.

She could feel the old woman's one good eye burrowing into her. "Are ye by chance a Chattan?" the shopkeeper asked.

"Ross," Annie said. "My father was born somewhere down the road," she added, quite a bit distracted.

"Raigmore?" the woman persisted.

Annie met her gaze. The color of her eye was a little brighter than Annie's, but green just the same. "Dunno. How much is this crystal?"

A tiny wry smile curved the old woman's lips. "'Tisna for sale, lass. As I said, 'tis precious."

Annie blinked, noting the orange price stickers on *all* the other crystals in the basket. Annoyed, she set the crystal down again, and managed to refrain from asking why it was in the basket to begin with if the woman didn't intend to sell it.

"However…I've a feeling ye were meant to have it," the shopkeeper announced before Annie could turn away.

Annie's brow furrowed. If it was an attempt to wrangle more money out of the silly tourist, it wasn't going to work. She wasn't exactly your normal tourist anyway. "Thanks. I'm no longer interested," she lied.

"Ach, ye mistake me, lass." The shopkeeper hurried over to pick the crystal up out of the basket and reached across the counter, handing it to Annie. In the woman's hands the striations seemed to turn green again. "'Tis yours for the taking, if ye'll have it."

Still Annie hesitated, not entirely certain she understood. But the scientist in her did a tiny little leap of glee. "You're giving it to me?"

The woman nodded. "If ye wish."

"But I thought—"

"The Winter Stone chooses who it wishes to keep it, it chooses ye."

Annie stared at the crystal in the shopkeeper's hand, blinking. The color now seemed to bleed into the rest of the crystal and even outside its translucent casing, casting a slight green hue on the woman's face in the dim light of the shop. The shopkeeper's green eye appeared all the greener by its light. *Perfectly bizarre.* Still Annie didn't reach out to take it yet, because she couldn't ascertain any logical reason why the woman would simply give it to her.

"Really?"

The woman nodded, her twinkling gaze almost as unnerving as the changing colors of the crystal.

Still insisting that she take it, the woman pushed it closer and Annie finally accepted it. "Thanks," she said. "That's sweet of you." But the instant she wrapped her hand about the crystal, she felt a sudden jolt down the length of her arm, and the crystal's colors altered sharply to shades of red and pink and back to green. Startled, Annie's gaze flicked back to the shopkeeper's.

The woman lifted a wiry white brow. "Fae magic," she offered with a wink.

Annie might have laughed at the explanation…she *might* have…if she could have formed a single rational thought over the reaction—hardly imagined, because the shopkeeper had witnessed it as well. It hadn't hurt, really, just a little zap like she sometimes got from static, only slightly stronger. "You should let me pay you," Annie insisted, a little dumbfounded.

"I dinna need your money, lass." The woman released the crystal into Annie's keeping. "No' everyone sees what ye see when ye peer into the keek stane."

"Keek stane?"

"An auld word for a scrying stone, crystal ball."

Annie smiled. "So what do I see?" she asked, testing the woman.

The woman tilted her head and seemed to think over her answer a moment, then said, "Truth, lies, and the destinies of men."

Annie lifted both her brows and gave the woman a half smile. "All that, eh?"

The shopkeeper smiled knowingly. She must have sensed Annie was waffling, because she added, "Take it and see what I mean, lass. If ye dinna wish to keep it, ye can bring it back before the first new moon."

Annie's lips found a smile of their own accord, but fortunately she didn't laugh at the woman's gypsy-speak. "Okay, well…I would love to take a closer look, but I'm only in town for a few weeks." She was too curious to turn down the offer, but she probably wouldn't feel right keeping it after all. "Do you have a card? I can mail it back when I'm done."

"If ye truly wish it, the Winter Stone will return on its own."

The woman was serious. Her ancient, withered face didn't crack a smile. Annie had a ridiculous vision in her mind of the crystal sprouting feet and walking back to the shop all by itself. Nevertheless, excited by the prospect of examining the crystal closer, she felt titillated by the offer. As odd as the entire situation might be, there was not much chance she would walk away without it. The scientist in her simply wouldn't allow it. "Alright." she agreed, but let me at least buy one of your tartan ponchos—how much did you say they were?"

"Forty nine, ninety nine, but it's on sale today. I'll gi' it to ye for twenty nine."

"Pounds?"

"Yes, of course!" the woman declared, and hurried over to pull the tartan poncho off the mannequin in the window. "Here ye go, lass. 'Twill serve ye well," she said, and Annie paid her. Then, thank God, she heard the rev of a bike engine outside the shop, and her cousin's boisterous voice, so she thanked the shopkeeper profusely and hurried outside.

Her cousin was still mounted on her bike, her short black skirt hiked up her leg to such a degree that Annie suffered a momentary pang of modesty at the thought of climbing on the back of the bike. The poncho would help at least.

Dressed all in black, from her shiny heeled boots to her black nails and purple lipstick, Kate was a beacon for every pair of male eyes in the vicinity. "Coorie up!" her cousin demanded. "We dinna ha' much time!"

"Check this out." Annie handed her the crystal while she pulled on her poncho.

Kate revved her bike with one hand as she examined the crystal. "What aboot it?"

"It changes colors."

In her cousin's hands, the crystal turned pink, but Kate didn't seem to notice. "Yer daft." she exclaimed, and shoved it back at Annie. "Get your bum on the bike. I've got a date." She beamed. "This time it's true love."

"Every one is true love for you!"

Kate gave her a chiding look. "Would ye even know love if ye were faced with it, Annie?"

Annie frowned at her. "*Anyway,* I thought you had to get back to work?"

Kate winked. "Why d' ye think I took the gig for, love? I'm working it."

Annie laughed and took the crystal from her cousin, dropping it into her pack. She climbed on the back of the bike and barely had time to adjust her pack and put her arm around her cousin's waist before Kate revved the bike and took off.

The wind tore strands of hair from Annie's ponytail, whipping them into her face. Houses whizzed past as they raced out of town, leaving the sounds of the Heritage Festival in their wake. Kate turned onto Ruthven and somewhere along that road veered off down another narrow road. About forty-five minutes later, after nearly three spills, Annie insisted Kate drop her off beyond the last walk-about parking. There were only two cars here today. Hopefully, she wouldn't run into other hikers. She slid off the bike, eager to be off Kate's wild bike ride.

"You sure you'll be alright?" Kate asked.

"Fine," Annie insisted.

"Okay, but if ye'll wait until t'morrow, I'll come along w' ye."

Annie shook her head stubbornly. "You don't have the gear."

"'Tis no' like ye're climbing the Alps, mind ye. I've got boots." Kate's full lips turned into a grin and she hiked up her leg to show off her shiny black boots with the deadly heels.

Little wonder they had nearly kissed the ground. How could anyone ride with those? Annie laughed. "Great, we can use them as grappling hooks," she suggested.

"Bloody hell! Ye're a stubborn one," Kate protested, but she laughed too. "Anyway, it's not like ye're rock climbing. It's a lazy day walk aboot at best."

Annie lifted a brow. "Thirty point nine kilometers if you do the entire pass."

"Aye, but ye're not," Kate argued.

"Right. So I'll hold you to it—tomorrow—but I'm going today too."

"Alright, then. Meet me back here at six. Set your watch," Kate insisted.

Annie didn't wear a watch. Apparently her cousin hadn't noticed, but she said anyway, "I will." She planned to be back long before Late Kate turned up again.

Tugging her enormous bag off Kate's bike, she watched in horror as the buckle in her strap caught her cousin's crocheted pullover. Thankfully, it released its hold without rending her cousin's flimsy sweater.

"Dinna fash yourself," Kate insisted. "If I'm lucky,

it'll meet the same fate at Russell's hands." Annie laughed again and Kate grinned. "We'll fix ye up t'morrow, love. It's aboot time ye took that stick out of your arse and lived a wee bit."

Annie threw her bag over her shoulder. "I didn't come here for that," she said. "I don't need a man in my life—or new clothes—or a new haircut, but thanks anyway, Kate. I know you mean well."

"Aye, ye do," Kate persisted. "Be back here at six," she reiterated, and then took off without giving Annie a chance to stand her ground.

Apparently, her cousin had already decided she was withering away after her breakup with Paul. But Annie was fine—more than fine. In fact, she was doing *exactly* what she wanted to do.

She watched as her cousin nearly took another spill, somehow saving herself as she turned and then zoomed past again, leaving Annie in her dust. *Literally.* Annie spat dust, and closed her eyes to ease the sting in her eyes. Kate was a trip—in a good way. However, they couldn't be more different, she decided as her cousin's brilliant mass of curls disappeared around the bend. The instant Annie was alone, she felt her tension melt away as she sucked in a breath of fresh air. And then she started on her way, eager to begin.

This time of the day, the sun had burned off most of the morning fog. The hills were a lovely string of emerald pearls. Most hikers just walked the Lairig Ghru pass, but this wasn't a full-on hike as Kate had pointed out. Annie only needed a clear view of the area from somewhere up high, so she took a route west. The wind was mild today, and it was sunny. A perfect day for hiking. Still, she was glad for the poncho, because it was a bit brisk.

What do I see?
Truth, lies and the destinies of men.

Bullshit, Annie thought. Still she itched to take the crystal out of her bag for another look. However, she had much too much ground to cover to stand here ogling a rock. And yet she felt its presence acutely, like a force of energy emanating from the depths of her pack.

Determined to forget it for the time being, she adjusted the pack at her back, pleased that she had found her day pack at such a great price. She might not be much into Coach or Louis Vuitton but she *loved* her new day pack. If there was one thing she felt passionate about it was good gear.

Estimating that she had a good six or seven hours before she needed to be back at the meeting point, she abandoned the road and found herself climbing mostly on rutted tracks. The pass was clear for most of the hike, but higher up in the rockiest terrain it was a bit more difficult to traverse, especially during winter when the entire pass was snowbound. The last time she'd hiked through with Paul, they had taken the Lairig Ghru straight through from Speyside to Deeside. Today, she would play it by ear. As she'd told Kate, there would be plenty of time to cover all the ground she needed to cover during the next few weeks, with far more planning once all of her gear arrived from wherever the airline had decided to ship it.

Normally, she was prepared for everything, but for once in her life it felt good to take it as it came. She had a cellphone for emergencies, she had a sandwich, her notebook and her camera—and she had her Farbgel—Scotland's answer to pepper spray—just in case—at Kate's insistence, of course. But she wasn't worried. The area was quite familiar to her, and it wasn't her first time out. In fact, she felt as though she had been born in these hills. Today company would only have slowed her down. Plus, she really didn't want to tell anyone what she was after—not yet.

Only her father would have understood.

She was excited by this. Of all the bait and switch theories, this was the only one that hadn't been thoroughly pursued, probably in part due to the fact that the stone was "home" now after having been returned to Scotland in 1996. The Kingussie report had surfaced about the same time the stone had returned to Scotland. Apparently, some old woman on her deathbed claimed her brothers had stumbled into a cave while playing up in the hills as boys and there they had discovered a stone that sounded a lot like the Stone of Destiny. Unfortunately, her brothers were both dead now too—one killed in World War II and the other fell off a ladder in his hardware store and cracked his skull at the age of sixty-two. Neither was around to corroborate the woman's story, but it didn't matter. Annie only needed something a more solid to go on in order to ask for an official dispensation—a long-buried cave, maybe. That was why she was heading up to the "Demon's Penis" today…to find her *proof*. After all, she didn't need any special permission to hike these hills or to poke about unofficially, and if there were unexplored caverns in the area, she was bound and determined to find them.

About an hour into her hike, she stopped at a burn, grateful that she'd worn her good hiking boots on the plane. Despite what Kate said, hiking the Cairngorms wasn't for the fainthearted, even when you stuck to well-worn paths. Crossing the burn at the footbridge, she headed west until the peak of *Bod an Deamhain* greeted her like an old friend in the distance. The munro leaned to one side, looking far more like a woman's breast than a demon's penis, but the sight of it filled Annie with an unparalleled sense of satisfaction, even as it brought back bittersweet memories of hiking with her parents.

While most parents might not have dragged their eight-year-old along on a hiking trip through some of the wildest terrain in Scotland, her father hadn't blinked an eye, nor had her mother—which was entirely to be expected considering that her dad had climbed some of the most challenging peaks on the face of the earth and her mother had met the love of her life traveling the Trans-Siberian. Her parents had been fearless. They'd instilled the same attitude in Annie. The simple fact that they had jumped out of planes together, taken a sailboat out for six months on the Pacific and met the Dalai Lama twice, made their deaths feel all the more senseless. Run down by a drunk driver only three blocks from her grandmother's house. On the way to pick her up, no less.

But, like her obsessions, Annie came by her sense of adventure honestly. She supposed that was why Paul had found it so difficult to deal with her. He said she was stubborn, opinionated and too independent. How could anyone be too independent? And how the hell did that give him the right to sleep with her best friend? How cliché. He hadn't even had the sense to cheat on her in an entirely original way. But the worst of it was that Annie had realized afterward how few true friends she actually had. Her life had been too wrapped up in her work, and if she got this new dig, that wasn't about to change. But that was fine. Moving to Scotland would be a good change. Spending more time with Kate would be great as well.

Today the walk was clearing her head, doing her good. In fact, by the time she emerged from the smattering of trees at the base of the corries, she already felt like a new woman. Up ahead, bright purple hues drew her inexorably toward them. On either side of the worn path bluebells sprang from the ground, swaying gently with the summer breeze.

Up higher, the hillside felt spongy beneath her boots. These were not your typical mountains, more like elevated plateaus. The name itself, Cairngorms, was a misnomer. Translated from Gaelic, it meant "blue cairn." However, made primarily of granite, the hills glowed red under the afternoon sun…a bit like the Winter Stone. It was why the old ones had named them the red hills—the *Am Monadh Ruadh.*

Stopping in the middle of a blooming field, she paused to take a look around. From here, she could spy the pine forest she'd come through down below. Sad to know that was all that was left of those amazing woodlands. Her stomach grumbled, so she picked a spot near a crumbling cairn, and pulled off her dry sack, then slid down to sit on the mossy ground, resting her back against a large boulder.

She must have been walking a good two hours or more, and she wasn't anywhere near where she needed to be. To check the time, she took her cell phone out of her bag. *2:15.* Okay, three hours, maybe a little more. She'd lost track. At this point, she'd be pushing it to get back to the meeting point by six, so she texted Kate to let her know her E.T.A. Then she fished her sandwich out of her bag, and along with it the Winter Stone, feeling a bit gleeful to be alone with her newfound treasure at last.

When she touched the crystal, the striations turned green.

Curioser and curioser.

Inspecting it as she finished her sandwich, she grabbed her canteen, took a sip of water, and then tossed everything but the stone aside to take a closer look at her prize…

CHAPTER TWO

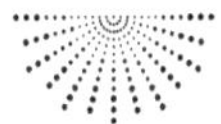

THE CAIRNGORMS, 878

Callum placed another rock on his father's burial cairn. The corries were littered with them—some said dropped by Cailleach Bheur herself—faerie tales, like those told by Kenneth MacAilpín. Except that those were harmless, and the lies Kenneth told were not.

He was angry with his Da for dying—angry with him for leaving him alone with decisions that weren't his to make.

MacAilpín's sons were all treacherous, murdering bastards—but this wasn't Callum's fight. Callum had followed his Da into these hills, because...well, that's what sons were supposed to do. But his father was barely cold in the ground and his uncle was already campaigning to return to Scone with the stone.

Apparently, loyalty was a dying trait.

And yet Callum could hardly fault his uncle Brude. In truth, he was wavering as well—more than a wee bit if the truth be known. Sweating under the hot afternoon sun, he placed the last of the cairn stones on his father's grave and stood with arms akimbo to inspect his handiwork. He had refused the help of his clansmen. This task was his alone. In part because he suspected treachery, but neither did he wish for anyone to witness his grief. It was a terrible thing, gnawing painfully at his guts.

His father had been the last of his blood. His mother was gone, his brothers as well—both victims of King Giric's coup—and now his Da was dead as well. There was no one to return to Scone for, no one to stay here for, and by the sins of Sluag, if a mon wasna fighting for his kin, who the hell was he fighting for in the end? The situation soured his mood.

Even now his kinsmen were down in the vale, arguing over what to do with the Destiny Stone. Half of his clan wanted to return the stone to Scone. The other half were more inclined to never allow it to see the light of day. Brude was the most vocal, wishing to return it, but that came as little surprise, for, like Callum, his uncle had never relished taking on this burden. As far as Callum was concerned, they could smash the stone to bits, return it, or leave it in the belly of the mountain. The rotten thing was cursed anyway.

But then they knew that, his Da would have said. That's why they had stolen the bloody thing to begin with, leaving a perfect replica in its place. Let them crown their kings upon that other slab of stone and mayhap it would stem rivers of blood.

Disgusted to his core, Callum turned away from the cairn. It was complete now, but he could not credit that his father's body would now lie and rot beneath the heavy stones. His bones would remain here for eternity, forgotten under the mists of *Am Monadh Ruadh.*

And where might Callum be?

Except for those who had followed his Da, his

tribesmen were now scattered to the winds. Alba was no more. He was a man without a home.

With a growl of displeasure, he started down the hillside, battling his conscience and his temper. That's when he spied her...

Annie yawned and stretched, thinking that somehow, she must have dozed...with the crystal in her hand. She lifted it to her bleary eyes. It was nearly colorless again. What a strange, but fascinating rock.

After eating her sandwich, she had been so entranced with the thing, peering into it, watching the colors change and trying to figure out how it worked, that she must have dozed. She didn't recall feeling sleepy, but she guessed it must have come upon her suddenly, after filling her stomach, because she *felt* like she'd been asleep for a hundred years or more. She thought maybe her plane trip must have taken more out of her than she had realized, because the hike hadn't been all that strenuous. She sat up and shook the fuzz from her head.

What time was it anyway?

Instinctively, she sought her bag to grab her phone and text Kate again, but her brand-new pack was gone. With a shriek of alarm, she shot to her feet, looking about, her gaze focusing on movement in the near distance.

There was a half-naked man, rebuilding the cairn she'd passed on the way up. Clearly, he must have taken her bag, because unlike the Winter Stone, bags didn't simply get up and walk away on their own. Wrapping her fist around the crystal in her hand, she was angry enough to whack the guy upside the head with it, so she took a few calming breaths before starting in his direction. At the very least, she needed her phone back so she could let Kate know she wasn't going to make it back on time.

And her camera. She'd spent half a month's salary on the bloody thing and she wasn't about to let some half-naked man have it.

Of course, she wanted her special pen, too—the one she'd been carrying around since she learned she'd gotten into the University of Michigan—her father's alma mater.

And maybe a hairband. She'd taken her hair down, but it was bugging her now.

And her map. She was pretty sure that if she covered enough ground she could find the Lairig Ghru pass and make her way back from there, but she would much rather get her bearings right here and now.

Damn it. She wanted her pack back—with all its contents! It wasn't so much that the bag was expensive, but it was perfect. It had taken her years to find a bag so right, and she didn't intend to give it up so easily. If he didn't return it, she vowed to knock him silly with this lovely rock. She gripped it harder within her fist, ready to do battle.

But the closer she got to the cairn, the more disoriented she felt—as though somehow she wasn't exactly in the same place where she'd sat down to eat her sandwich. She faltered, looking around.

Where was she? The mountain peaks were all in the right places, but something wasn't right here. The trees were closer—as though they'd crept up the mountain while she wasn't looking.

She turned back to the man who was busy defacing the cairn. Dressed as he was, there was clearly no place for him to have hidden her bag on his person, but he could have buried it beneath the rocks. Didn't he realize these things were of historical significance? He was defacing history! He was making it nearly impossible for someone who knew what they were doing to come in and make any sense of the structure.

Naked bastard.

"What do you think you're doing?" she asked when he turned suddenly to face her.

For an instant, he looked bemused by the sight of her, but quickly recovered and narrowed his gaze. "Burying my da," he replied sourly. "Not that 'tis any o' your bloody concern, wench. Where di' ye come from?"

Annie automatically turned to examine her surroundings, as perplexed by the question as he seemed to be by her presence.

Bod an Deamhain was unmistakable in the distance. There it was. And she thought maybe she was halfway up Cairn Toul but couldn't swear by it...everything was different.

Once again she faced the half-naked Scotsman. His clothes weren't all that tailored. In fact, he was only wearing a blanket—sort of. His legs were bare except for some crude strappy leather sandals that climbed his massive calves. And his chest was bare too, his bit of a blanket wrapped crudely about his waist, like some sad imitation of a great kilt.

He took her measure in turn, examining her curiously from her ten-year-old utilitarian boots to her cousin's skirt and poncho—obviously not much impressed with what he saw. Annie tried not to be offended by his sour expression. Okay, so the skirt might not look as hot on her as it did on Kate, but no one had ever looked at her quite like *that*—as though she were a mutated cell under a microscope.

"If ye're a spy for the crown," he announced, "ye might as well hie yourself back to Scone! Ye ha' no quarrel from my people, but we no longer ha' any interest in aligning ourselves with the sons of MacAilpín."

Annie blinked. She understood just enough to know the man was a bit of a loon. A gorgeous loon, but a loon nonetheless. But hey, even gorgeous people went nuts. For an instant, she wondered if maybe he had escaped from nearby St. Vincent's. As far as she knew the hospital dealt mostly with psychiatric patients. Bu—she turned to look around once more—they weren't exactly within walking distance.

"I was…uh…looking for my bag," Annie said, her anger much deflated. "Have you seen it…by chance?"

"Bag?"

The lass nodded. "Blue. A dry sack. Sea to Summit. Probably overkill, but it's the best I've ever had. I want it back."

Callum couldn't be certain, but he thought she might be accusing him of stealing her purse. I dinna have your pouch—dry nor wet—an' I ha' no bloody idea what the hell you're on aboot." Callum tried not to look at her bare legs. All that saved her arse from hanging out for all the world to see was the mean cloak she had flung over her head. Save that he didn't see any obvious tearing of the material, he thought mayhap her clothes must be rent and ruined. "What manner of clothing do ye wear, lass? Were ye beset upon by brigands?"

The wind picked up, tossing her shiny black hair, lifting up the strange tartan with a hole for her head, revealing a tiny, but well-sewn skirt beneath the cloak that scarce covered her minge. "Not that it's any of your bees wax," she said. "But it's my family's plaid."

He scratched his head. "Ach, lass! I hate to tell ye, but there's scarce enough for ye alone, much less your entire family." If, in truth, it was her poor family's tartan, they'd be spendin' a mighty cauld winter. Callum felt a moment's pity for the lass.

She had the audacity to look at him as though he were the one who was daft—this woman who spoke of killing blue sacks from sea to summit. Her brows collided fiercely and her eyes crossed. She seemed unable to speak suddenly, and her mouth hung open as though she meant to say a thing, but couldn't find the words.

Callum placed a hand to his hip. "So ye would ha me believe ye were simply wanderin' aboot, searching for some god-forsaken blue purse?"

She found her tongue again, with about as much pluck as any woman he'd ever encountered. "Yes! It has my cell, and I want it back! Right now!"

"Ye carry a cell in a purse? What manner of witchery be that, wench?"

"What the hell are you talking about?" the lass exploded. Her cheeks turned a vivid shade of pink that was nicely complimented by her dark, shiny hair. She wasn't a lay about, he didn't believe, because her skin was kissed golden by the sun.

Callum screwed his face. "Ye're a pawky wench. I saw *no* bag lying aboot, and I dinna believe ye anyhow. Ye dinna hail from my kinsmen and ye canna simply have come traipsing up the ben all by yourself with a cell in your bloody purse." His hand went to the hilt of the dagger in his belt. "Tell me now afore I take your head—where are your murderous, thieving kinsmen?"

The woman took a step back, startled, it seemed, and it was then he noticed the small round crystal in her hand. Her fist was curled about it as though she meant to use it to strike him. Every time the wind lifted her plaid, Callum found his gaze shifting to her tiny skirt. Her legs were long, lean and lovely. By their sacred stone, in that instant, she might have hit him with her bloody rock, and for all his bluster, he didn't truly care. If she managed to knock him out, mayhap she would knock some sense into his head, so that he might better know what to do with his quibbling kinsmen and that accursed stone in their possession.

"I'm no thief!" she countered angrily. "But I've always heard it takes one to know one," she shot back at him.

Callum scratched his head. Shaking himself free of the distraction of her legs, he asked, "So ye're confessing as much, are ye?"

She seemed taken aback by the question. "What! I'm confessing nothing!" The woman's hands went to her hips and her expression appeared as stormy as the clouds that were suddenly rolling in overhead. The breeze whipped again, kicking up the hem of her measly skirt and Callum blinked as he caught sight of tiny red breeches. These were strange, strange garments she wore, but no stranger than her speech. She swept past him suddenly her black hair lashing furiously at her back as she moved toward the cairn he'd labored so hard to build. "You're the thief!" she accused him outright, and then suddenly, she was undoing all his hard work, disinterring his Da.

"Oh, nay ye dinna!" On any other day Callum might have mustered some patience, not today. "Bloody hell, wench!"

He wasn't in the mood. The weather here was as fickle as a whore in a room full of rich men and he wasn't about to stand by and let her undo all his hard work—nor stand here arguing while the sky emptied down upon their heads. This was the most changeable weather he had ever known—unpredictable as a woman's temper. She didn't respond at once, so he plucked her up and put her over his shoulder and turned and started down the mountain.

Annie shrieked in protest. "Put me down!"

"Nay," the man said much too calmly.

"Hey!" Annie smacked him once upon the back. "You can't just pick me up and carry me off like some savage!"

He said nothing to that, simply continued to make his way down the hill and the cairn grew smaller as they marched away from it. Above them, the sky was darkening, clouds swirling around the peak of *Bod an Deamhain*. The blanket the man was wearing whipped up in the breeze, rewarding Annie with an eye-full of his ass—a nice, muscular ass, but that was beside the point.

"Hey!" she screamed again. "This is two thousand fourteen! You can't just carry women away like this!"

Still he didn't respond, simply marched down the hill without a word, and remembering the crystal in her hand, she whacked him once more on the back, as hard as she could.

He growled like a bear and tossed her down on the ground, knocking the air out of her lungs. Annie dropped the crystal.

CHAPTER THREE

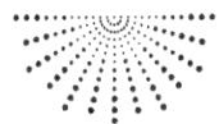

Callum's first instinct had been to toss the girl, but he regretted that at once. She lay before him crumpled like a broken flower. He had never once abused a woman in all his days. In truth, there was not a female in his clan who would stand for him daring to carry her away like a sack of meal, but she'd vexed him with her strange words and her ridiculous accusations.

He glared down at her.

Her skirt had flown up, revealing tiny red breeches that were so wee they didn't actually cover her buttocks. In fact, they disappeared like a string into the crack of her arse and he wondered if the lass were far too poor to afford more cloth. Her pristine white tunic was full of grass stains, and her hair was tangled in her useless cloak, covering her face. Her boots, oddly made, had seen better years.

He lifted up the crystal that rolled to his feet, and before she could regain her senses, he lifted her up as well.

"I've nay wish to harm ye, lass, but ye'll be answerin' to my kin." She groaned in protest as he tossed her over his shoulder once more. But he warned her, "Dinna think to do that again. I've been told my head is as hard as the stones in these hills and I'll warrant all ye'll manage to do is sour my mood."

It took Annie a befuddled instant to regain her bearings.

"*Me* sour *your* mood?" she asked. "You're the one who stole my bag, defaced public property, and then lifted me up like some Neanderthal!"

"I've told ye, I ha'na seen your bloody dry sack, woman! And I dinna understand a word ye say. What tongue is that ye speak?"

"Me?" she shrieked. "You! I don't understand *anything* you're saying! Don't you know English when you hear it?"

"English!"

Without warning, he hurled her down once more. Thank God the hillside was soft and spongy, breaking Annie's fall, not her bones. Also quite fortunately, she missed a crop of rocks. That would have hurt.

"Bloody English!" he exclaimed. "I should ha' known. That explains your idiocy, wench! What are ye doing aboot these parts?"

The impact knocked the breath from Annie's lungs. She groaned, rolling to her back. At the instant, she didn't care that her legs were turned up to the sky and her skirt was flapping in the wind. The sky had turned so quickly it—it was true, if you didn't like the weather in Scotland, just wait five minutes.

"First of all," she began, once her breath returned and she could talk again. "I'm American. *Not* English." His murderous glare turned abruptly to one of confusion. When it didn't appear he was going to pounce on her again, she sat and tried to explain. "My dad was Scottish. Mother American. Both dead now. Why am I telling you this? I don't even know you!"

His look softened a bit at her revelation, but his stance remained threatening.

The wind whipped around them, snapping his crude blanket like a weathered flag. Annie groaned. She had the strangest feeling suddenly…as though she were not quite anchored in reality. She examined him closer…maybe for the first time. His long black hair was braided at the sides, probably to keep the hair out of his face. It certainly wasn't a fashion statement. His eyes were the color of steel, but they appeared nearly as confused as Annie felt.

As absurd as it seemed, after tossing her down twice, she had the sense he wouldn't do her any real harm.

She took another glance around, noticing the subtle differences in the landscape. The cairn in the distance was newly built, not eroded. The grass was no longer quite as green as it had appeared when she'd sat down to eat her sandwich. The bluebells were gone.

Same place.

Not the same time.

How could this be?

She turned back to her barbarian friend. Although she knew it must be impossible, he seemed to be the real deal. And no, he wasn't crazy. Nothing about that look in his eyes was crazed. In fact, it was the single most knowing gaze she had ever met in all her life. He was assessing her quietly, listening, standing with arms akimbo, eyes narrowed, waiting for her to continue.

Oh, God...there was no way...no way...no way...

Annie's heart skipped a beat as she considered testing him. Languages were her love, and the ancient Scots tongue in particular was her forte.

"*Cò às an do tharraing thusa?*" she blurted. *Where have you come from?*

His dark brows lifted in surprise, but he replied.

"Sgàin. A bheil gàidhlig agaibh?" Scone. You speak the old tongue?

No way, no way, Annie kept repeating in her head. Some folks still spoke Gaelic in these parts. And the language wasn't that far removed. It proved nothing, but she answered anyway, *"Tha, rud beag." Yes, a little.*

"Cò stiùir thu an seo?" Who sent you here?

"Chan eil. An tòir airClach na Cinneamhain." Nobody. I'm seeking the Destiny Stone.

Without warning, his temper exploded yet again. *"Mac Bhàdhair fhuileach thu!"Son of a cow's bloody afterbirth!* He threw his hands into the air and advanced upon her, his look murderous.

"Oh God!" Annie exclaimed, scrambling backward in the grass. She realized two things in that frightening instant. First, the guy was suddenly really and truly pissed. And second, she wasn't in Kansas anymore—not literally or figuratively.

CHAPTER FOUR

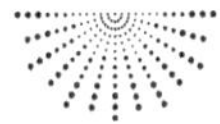

Where she was, precisely, Annie didn't know.

The lake and surrounding area looked a lot like Loch Einich, but if, in fact, that's where they were right now, none of the constructions she spied now were evident in present day.

She sat, reeling, trying to determine how she'd come to be here—not in the vale, of course. She knew exactly how she'd gotten here: Her half-naked Scot had produced a gnarly knife and then had marched her down the hill at the tip of his blade, cursing roundly at her back. At least she thought they were curses. Her repertoire of the ancient Scots language stopped short of profanity, but his tone revealed more than enough.

They didn't walk very far. His *kin* were camped near a lake, surrounded by construction in various stages, as though they had only arrived at this place. Or maybe they were preparing to leave after ravaging this poor village. He *had* been constructing a cairn, after all.

That thought gave her a bit of a shiver.

She knew this area well enough, despite that it had been years since her last visit with Paul. In present day, there were no permanent signs of these dwellings. No excavations had recorded any evidence of this type—at least none that she knew of. Still, that's where she believed she *must* be—Loch Einich. She could tell by the position of the surrounding mountains.

As inconceivable as it seemed, she *had* fallen asleep —like Rip Van Winkle—but instead of waking up one hundred years into the future, she had slipped into the distant past. Her brain attempted to form a coherent and logical explanation for that, but she couldn't seem to allow herself to accept her suspicions. However, with every passing minute and every word uttered, she suspected more and more it was true.

Eight men and women were gathered around the fire where her Scot had deposited her, but there were a number of others in the vicinity as well. These particular eight were especially intimidating—including the two women. Dressed in clothing that gave Annie the distinct impression they were prepared to do battle—with knives tucked into every loop and boot—they appeared ready, not just to slice her throat, but each other's as well. These were *not* re-enactors, she sensed. It was doubtful she had stumbled upon some lost clan living secretly in the Cairngorms. As wild as these hills might seem, they drew hikers all year long. Up until the time she'd gotten engaged, she'd made them a yearly sojourn.

It was twilight. The sun was setting over the distant hilltops. Beautiful, but a chill was rising in the air. Not even the poncho she'd bought this morning seemed to be keeping her warm.

Had she truly bought it only this morning?

The tag was still hanging off the fringe, but at this point, with her nervous kneading, she had nearly rubbed out the ink. The shopkeeper had been right, although now Annie had to wonder about that odd look the old woman had given her—as though she had known.

Because she *had* known, Annie realized.

The more she thought about it, the more she knew it was true. What else had the shopkeeper said?

The Winter Stone chooses who it wishes to keep it...it chooses ye.

In fact it *had* exhibited physical changes to Annie's touch.

Fae magic, the woman had proclaimed after the crystal had given Annie a rude shock.

Could it be?

She'd had a car once—a Jeep—that had shocked her every time she'd touched it. She'd joked often that it didn't like her, but that was metal, and there was no explanation why she'd experience such a shock from what amounted to no more than a ball of glass.

But magic?

While standing in the shop, Annie vividly recalled wishing with all her heart that she could see this place a thousand years ago...well, here she was. The scientist in her was fascinated, but then a thought occurred to her: What if this wasn't reversible?

If ye dinna wish to keep it," she heard the old woman's voice say in her head. *"Bring it back before the first new moon.*

Bloody hell! as Kate would say.

Presumably, she must be holding the damned thing. Unfortunately, at the moment she was sitting with her wrists bound, trying to eavesdrop while they argued over her fate—something they didn't appear to agree on. Annie could feel the tension mounting in every word bandied between them. Callum—her half naked Scot—had her crystal.

The entire clan spoke the same Scots tongue, but they looked more like she imagined the Picts might have looked. Some were painted with woad—the women as well. And she noticed Callum had a gnarly wolf head woad tattoo on his back. In fact Callum seemed to be the leader, though he was clearly at odds with some guy she overheard him call Brude.

Brude was a large, obnoxious man, with a long beard sporting twin braids. He had a penchant for resting his hand below his chin while he listened, clutching the dirty beard in his fist like a bell pull. He too had a wolf painted on his chest.

Every so often, one of the eight would peer in Annie's direction with a ferocious glare. Apparently she had stumbled upon them at a *very* inopportune time. Their chieftain was dead, possibly even murdered. But they were also hiding something. *Something important.* Something they had apparently stolen from Scone…

Annie blinked as another inconceivable thought popped into her head.

Could it be?

But, no!

And yet he had tossed her like a caber when she'd mentioned the Stone of Destiny up on the hill. Could they be hiding the Destiny Stone?

Cripes—her head was suddenly reeling—she had actually come searching for the thing…but she had never expected to find it—not like this. Every word of their heated discourse seeped into her brain only reluctantly:

"Could they have discovered it missing by now?" one of the women asked, her voice somber. Dressed in much the same crude manner as the men, she wore homemade tats of fish.

"Nay," replied an elder man. "Unless someone has betrayed us, they canna know. Even the plaque we left was the same."

The pinewood in the fire crackled between them,

far enough away that its warmth merely teased Annie, and a weighted silence fell between them.

In the distance, she heard men and women murmuring low, as though interested in the fireside discussion, but unwilling to disturb what Annie surmised were their leaders.

Callum's voice was sober. "My father was hale enough when we left Scone," he interjected. Annie thought she detected suspicion in his tone, but it wasn't directed at anyone in particular.

"What say ye, Callum?"

Callum crossed his arms, still holding her Winter Stone, tucking away under his arm. "Only that no one else took ill over that meal."

"'Tis a serious matter. D' ye mean to accuse someone of poisoning Finn?"

Callum cast Annie a glance before turning to the man speaking. "I mean to accuse no one, Brude. And yet did I no' know every one o' ye here, I would in truth suspect poison, and then mayhap treachery o'er the stone as well. But there's no' a one of us who would benefit by siding with the sons of MacAilpín. Is there?"

The group remained silent at Callum's declaration.

"Of the elders only you, Uncle, wish to return the stone to Scone, though I canna see as how you or anyone else might benefit by murdering Finn."

Brude began to pace. He eyed another man with twisted bird heads painted on his body. "I am not the only one. For my part, I dinna believe we must suffer to live like monks to save those fools from themselves. Who gives a damn if they slay one another and their kin over Scotia's throne. I say return the stone, curse and all."

The woman interjected. "'Tis true. Brude is not the only one who wishes to leave here," she said pointedly.

"I distinctly recall *you* say you wished to leave as well, Callum."

"With one difference. I dinna give a damn about returning the stone. Ye can keep it here in the vale, smash it to bits, I dinna care." He cast Annie another glance. "Except that...now I am reconsidering..."

The intensity of his gaze unnerved her. Annie had to look away. She sat, listening, fiddling with the price tag on her poncho, as the twilight lowered into one of the darkest nights she had ever witnessed. After awhile, only the faces surrounding the fire were visible—entirely unnerving, with the firelight revealing angry faces...and the sky as black as she had ever seen it. But without city lights to brighten the horizon, this is how it would appear.

Be careful what you wish for, her father had often said.

Well, here it is, Dad. I wished it, and here it is.

Annie's brain hurt, and yet she came closer and closer to accepting the truth...somehow, she *had* fallen through time...to ancient Scotland...and these people... they had her Stone of Destiny. Only who were these people? And why did they have the Stone of Scone?

The elder of the two women cast a bitter glance toward Annie. "What aboot her?"

Callum eyed Annie as well. "What? The lass?"

"Aye, she could ha'e done it," one of the men, not Brude, suggested.

Callum rejected the idea out of hand. "Nay. She's as daft as they come. Besides, no Scoti would ever send a woman to do their dirty work. They are no' like us. They keep their women's bellies plowed with bairns and their mouths open long enough to suckle their cocks. At any rate...look at her...she's as poor as a beggar. She canna even afford enough material to finish her dress. Clearly she wasna bribed."

Annie bristled. She resisted the urge to speak out in

her own defense. She wasn't poor. She was frugal. There was a difference. Her boots might not be new, but they were good, solid boots. In fact, she'd spent more money to resole them once every few years than it would have cost her to buy new ones. Because she *liked* these boots!

"Her clothes appear new," Brude contended.

"Aye, well, ye'd keep yours pristine as well if ye had but a sliver to wash," Callum suggested.

Annie glared at him. Really, he was one to talk—with his bare ass hanging out. In fact, she had to look away now and again whenever he shifted on his perch so she couldn't see up the blanket he was wearing. But she said nothing. She wasn't about to give them any more ammo to do her any harm. That knife blade had had a serious edge, and they didn't appear to be softening in her behalf.

"Ach, didna she say she was a Scoti?" asked one of the women, stretching out her hand, asking for Annie's crystal.

Callum handed the Winter Stone to her. The glassy surface shone by the firelight as it passed into her hands. "Aye. She said she was English as well, and yet she speaks our tongue as though she were born to it."

Annie eyed the crystal longingly. Somehow, if she could get the darned thing back into her possession, she sensed it was the key to returning where she belonged. She didn't know how the thing worked, but she knew instinctively it was responsible for bringing her here. And evidently, she had to have it back by the first new moon—whenever that might be. She peered up at the black sky. The moon was half full at the instant, but she couldn't tell if it was waxing or waning.

What do I see? she'd asked the shopkeeper.

Truth, lies and the destinies of men.

"She also said she was searching for *Clach na Cin-*

neamhain," Brude pointed out. "How could she know about the Destiny Stone if she wasna a spy?"

Without warning, Callum turned toward Annie, his grey eyes reflecting the firelight with an eerie brilliance. "How di' ye know about *Clach na Cinneamhain?*"

Annie peered down at her bound hands, considering a smart retort. She also considered telling the truth—that she had been pursuing the stone's history academically for nearly twelve years now. She settled on a big-fat lie, taking a stab at what she knew of their culture. "Because I'm a faerie," she announced.

The looks on all their faces ranged from surprise, to fear and doubt. If Annie had been a little less unnerved by the entire situation, she might have laughed.

Callum's dark brows crashed, apparently disliking her answer. "Ye said ye were a Merican," he growled.

It wasn't a question, but Annie nodded. "That's where faeries come from. Have you not heard of America?"

"Nay! So ye're telling' me ye're a fae with a mortal father and mother?"

Annie was no expert on faeries, but she thought it could be possible. Honestly, right now, she was thinking practically anything could be possible. She shrugged, trying for a disaffected tone. "It happens to the best of us."

Callum narrowed his gaze.

Annie was desperate to get the crystal back now. "Look…if you'll just give me my crystal, I'll prove it to you." She couldn't tell what it might be doing at the instant, or what their reaction to it was. Their attention seemed far more riveted on Callum's discussion with her, but she hoped there might be some way to use the crystal to impress them. Kate hadn't appeared to see any color changes, but the shopkeeper clearly had. Did these people see it as well?

She hoped.

The one called Brude suddenly seized the crystal from the woman who was holding it. He loomed over the group, glaring into the gently glowing orb.

Even from where Annie sat, she could see that it was turning a shade of pink in his grasp, though he seemed oblivious to that fact. "What's so special aboot this piece o' shite rock?" he demanded.

Annie hitched her chin up at him, and said with a sort of gypsy flair, "*That,* sir, is the Winter Stone. In its depths I see truth, lies and the destinies of men!"

"Bollocks!" the bearded man exploded. Though even as he said it, red sparked in his hands, and Annie experienced a tiny jolt of excitement at the discovery. He was getting angry. That much was clear. Maybe his anger was affecting the crystal's color? It made sense to her in an odd sort of way. In many color association charts, red was attributed to anger. That, or passion, but then passion was also an intense emotion, she reasoned. If she could keep him talking, she might better be able to test the crystal. She had no clue what the colors meant as yet.

"I heard you say you buried your chief..." Her gaze was directed at Brude, not Callum now, though she realized it was Callum's father and she felt another stab of guilt for intruding on his moment up on the ridge.

It took Brude a long instant to reply, and during that time, the crystal's color heightened. "He was my brother," he admitted, but reluctantly, his face twisted with what appeared to be regret mixed with anger.

Nothing ventured, nothing gained. "Are you maybe pleased over his death?"

The crystal's color glowed brighter and he stood a little straighter, dropping the hand with the crystal at his side. He stiffened his shoulders as he scowled down at her. "What sort o' daft question is that?"

For his part, Callum remained quiet, watching curiously. She shrugged, trying not to show fear at Brude's aggression. "It was simply a question. I heard he was poisoned."

The look on the man's face turned murderous. "Are ye accusing me of killing my own brother, outlander bitch?"

Did faeries plead for their lives? Annie winced. "No."

He suddenly hoisted the crystal into the air, his voice thunderous. In his hand, the crystal glowed a fiery shade, illuminating his face with an eerie glow that set his forked beard afire. "I ought tae crack ye're skull!" he said. "Instead, I'll smash ye're bloody keek stane!" He lunged toward the boulder where Callum sat, clearly intending to smash the crystal.

Inconceivably, Callum didn't flinch as the brute descended upon him.

"No!" Annie cried, terrified that he would destroy her way home. "Please!"

Thankfully, Callum intervened. He stood, halting the man with a gently raised hand. "Enough!" he said.

The man froze above Callum, his expression full of fury.

Okay, so red was definitely anger, Annie decided, as Brude stood there, glaring at her with the crystal frozen in mid air. She couldn't believe no one else seemed to notice the red-hot orb—especially not Brude. Like a mini sun, it shed its light far beyond the reach of the fire.

With a lifted brow, Callum peered from Annie to the crystal. He stood and calmly removed it from his uncle's hand, then turned toward Annie, closing the distance between them, seeming not to notice the crystal's transformation as it faded to pink in his grasp. It remained pink as he stared at her, holding it for her to take.

Annie's heart was racing.

Awkwardly, because of the bindings on her wrists, she reached up to accept the crystal from him. To her surprise, as she touched it, that same arc of energy shot through her arm and she cried out, nearly dropping it. Somehow, she held onto it, and in her hands it turned to green.

Her reaction did not escape Callum's notice, but Brude was unfazed. "She's a lying bitch!" he groused as Annie recovered from the shock. "If she were a faerie—as she claims—she wadna still be sitting with arms bound. An' ye wadna be keeping the wench if the sight of her didna harden your greedy cock, Callum mac Finn!"

Annie gasped aloud, peering up in surprise to gauge Callum's reaction.

He was still staring at her, not at the crystal, nor at his uncle. And then he suddenly turned to address his kinsmen, and said evenly, "Until Biera arrives to give her a trial, whether ye like it or nay, the lass is under my protection." He peered back at Annie and reassured her, "No one will harm ye, lass, as long as I have breath. I may no' believe in faeries…but I believe in you."

CHAPTER FIVE

Those four little words kept echoing in Annie's head.

I believe in you.

Even more than "I love you," they had the power to infiltrate the little cracks of her heart. She sat mulling over the thrill it gave her to hear Callum say those words. But, really, why should she care if he believed in her? Aside from the simple fact that his *not* believing in her could prove to be life threatening, she didn't know this man. Whether or not he had faith in Annie, the person, shouldn't matter. And yet the simple fact that Paul had never believed in anything she had stood for—even after five years together—and this man had stood up for her after knowing her all of—what? A few hours?—was quite...confusing.

Point in fact: It had taken her all this time to even consider going after a dig for the Stone of Destiny. Why? Because her lovely fiancé had often pointed at her thesis, and her professor's comments, as proof that she was batty. He had made her feel invalidated, and the last trek they'd made through the Cairngorms, Annie had secretly scoped out the terrain, without saying a word to Paul about her intentions.

All of it was so bemusing.

At least she had the Winter Stone back in her possession. Except that now she had to figure out how to make it work. Apparently, simply wishing upon the crystal wasn't enough, despite the shopkeeper's claim. Though Annie clearly recalled her saying, *"If ye truly wish it, the Winter Stone will return on its own."So much for that.* It wasn't working, and it certainly couldn't be that she had reservations about leaving here—despite that little rush Callum's words had given her.

Right, so she'd prefer to hang around a bunch of barbarians instead of getting home and crawling into her nice warm bed?

No.

However, she conceded, just maybe the chance at seeing the Stone of Destiny was holding her back... maybe a little? It was possible, because she was probably willing to saw off a limb or two for that opportunity.

In her hand the crystal had grown cold and milky again. She set it down beside her, contemplating its strange properties—none of which could be properly explained by properties known to her. Annie believed all things worked within the laws of nature, yet clearly there must be something she was missing here.

She eyed the woman they had left to guard her. Half naked, just like Callum. Hair streaked with gray and similar braids. Woad, half worn off. Weird clothes. Nope. Annie would be willing to bet that woman hadn't seen a hairdryer in all her life.

Their discussion ended, the entire group had moved away from the fire, except for the elder woman. Someone came and dumped wood at the woman's side, and she fed the fire all the while eyeing Annie with a look of undisguised suspicion.

Apparently, they didn't trust her. How was she supposed to have guessed they were hiding the Stone of Destiny—less that she had somehow traversed centuries to arrive here at the perfect time to open mouth, insert foot?

The word coincidence didn't apply here. She sensed there was something far greater at work. No, this wasn't simply a coincidence.

Fae magic.

Had Annie somehow wished herself here while in that curio shop? Could it be that she had been so obsessed with *Lia Fàil* all her life because it had been her destiny all along? Maybe this was another one of those chicken or the egg riddles, because sitting here now, it felt strangely as though she had lived her entire life for this occasion, and that everything she had ever done had brought her to here and now.

She was still contemplating that when Callum returned, making his way purposely toward her, carrying something in his hand. He knelt beside her, surprising her with a napkin filled with foodstuffs. "Ye must be famished, lass?"

Annie peered up at him in surprise. Hungry? She had eaten her entire sandwich before falling asleep on that bloody hill and this situation wasn't exactly giving her an appetite. "I'd rather have my hands unbound," she said honestly. He frowned, but seemed to consider her request, so she pressed. "Please, where am I supposed to go? There's only one way out of this valley, and you have it guarded by thugs."

His brows collided. "Thugs?"

"Goons, gangsters..."

His expression only appeared all the more confused.

Annie sighed. "Guards."

"Ach, lass, why di' ye no' simply say so?" He set the napkin down beside her, and unsheathed the knife at his boot.

Annie lifted both her brows as she watched him saw at her ropes. She would have argued that she was "saying so," except that she was getting what she wanted so she held her tongue. "Thank you," she said instead as his knife sliced through the last of the rope. Already her wrists were chafed, after only a few hours of being bound, and she rubbed the raw area with her thumb.

He eyed her, a warning in his steel gray eyes. "Dinna disappoint me, lass. If ye attempt to escape, I canna promise to keep ye safe. D' ye ken?"

Annie nodded.

"Now eat," he demanded. "Ye're naught but skin and bones."

Annie nodded, hoping to appease him so he would go away and allow her to continue examining her crystal in peace—certainly not because the sight of him made her envision him naked. He was buff, but not in the same way as those gym-heads who posed in the gym mirrors. His body was strong and sculpted by what could only have been long hours of labor. Still, it wasn't like her to think of men as sex objects. She lifted a slab of cheese from the napkin, acutely aware of his scrutiny.

His eyes seemed to peer straight into her soul. "I'll bring ye a wee dram," he offered, though he sat down beside her, lifting his knees and wrapping his muscular arms around them, watching her nibble at the cheese. "Ye're a strange lass," he remarked after a moment. His lips broke into a boyish grin that made Annie's heart skip a beat. "Then again ye're one o' the fae, so ye would ha'e me believe..."

Quite certain of his answer, Annie asked, "Just how many faeries have you known? I'll have you know that everyone in America looks exactly like me."

He lifted a brow. "*Exactly?*"

"Okay, maybe not *exactly*."

His lips tipped at the corners, making Annie's heart trip a little harder. Men like him rarely paid attention to her. Men like him preferred her cousin Kate. "Sounds like a mon's idea of heaven," he said, surprising her, and Annie blinked, heat suffusing her cheeks.

"Are you flirting with me?"

Once again his brows drew together, as though he didn't quite understand. "Flirting?"

"Never mind," Annie said awkwardly. But he *was*, she realized. The man was flirting with her. She couldn't mistake that mischievous gleam in his eyes. Or the appreciative way he was looking at her…nor could she ignore that familiar pang of desire that was building somewhere deep inside.

Reluctant to leave the lass yet, Callum leaned back against the boulder they had *named Clach Tolargg,* in honor of their fallen brethren. His people believed these stones were the leavings of their gods. The greater the stone, the more significance it held, and the greater the spiritual connection. They held their counsels here.

"I need ye to tell me the truth, lass. Who sent ye? From whence di' ye come?"

She stiffened. "Okay…that makes sense." Her tone was full of reproach, and mayhap a bit of disappointment. She waved the cheese at him. "You want something from me, so you think you can flirt your way to answers." She gave him a lovely little impertinent nod and he found himself enchanted by the guileless gesture.

However, talking to her made his head ache—inconceivably, even more than the problem of the Destiny Stone. He raked a hand across his whiskers, and considered getting up again to fetch her that dram he'd promised—himself as well. He sorely needed it after the day he'd had. However, something kept him seated at her side.

He hadn't set out to "*flirt*" with the lass, as she'd called it, but he certainly did not find her wanting. While her dress was odd, her hair was shiny and straight, cascading about her shoulders like a mantle of black silk. Her brows, perfectly formed, arched over pale green eyes. And her lips were made for a mon to kiss. If in truth he believed in faeries, she might well be precisely how he'd envision one—with creamy skin as soft as butter and legs that made a mon think of having them wrapped about his waist. However, it would do her little good if his kinsmen thought he was protecting her simply because he wanted to appease his cock.

Auld Morag watched them closely.

He considered the girl a long moment, thinking that strangely enough, her appearance here in the vale had settled his restlessness. Admittedly the thought of spending his life here in the Mounth no longer seemed quite so devoid of possibilities...if the girl stayed as well.

"I need answers," he said, "and I intend to get them, but, nay, I dinna find ye appealing, if that's what ye mean. Ye're too skinny for my taste," he lied.

Annie frowned. He was lying, she was certain. She recognized desire, and it was right there in his steely eyes. "Whatever," she said and swallowed her bite of cheese.

"Tell me your name."

"Annie Ross."

"Annie Ross," he repeated.

It wasn't a question, Annie surmised. He seemed to be savoring the sound of her name—much like she was enjoying the bite of cheese he'd given her—judging by the mold, some kind of blue? She had never tasted anything quite like it—nor had she ever met a man quite like him. And he was acting a lot like a man with a hard-on. *He was a liar.*

"So ye hail from Ross-shire, then? Are ye Fidach by blood?" He fidgeted uncomfortably, and Annie decided to prove him wrong—of course, without stopping to question why she felt so safe with such a blatant flirtation. She shifted, lifting her knee to see if he would sneak a peek.

Fidach was a name she recognized, but she had no idea whether she was connected to the ancient clan. Oddly enough, despite her curious nature, and her obsession with the Stone of Destiny, she had never been driven to trace her clan's ancestry. "Fidach? As in the sons of Cruithne, King of the Picts?"

His look darkened considerably. "We are *seven* nations, *all* with royal blood. 'Tis a blasphemy we have taken the Pecht name. 'Tis no' our own." Annie was too shocked to be disappointed by the fact that he ignored her blatant invitation to peek up her skirt.

Cripes, she thought. *Callum is a Pict.*

I am talking to a Pict.

The crystal was suddenly forgotten at her side. So was her failed attempt at seduction. He had her rapt attention now. The Picts had mysteriously vanished from the annals of history. Her peers were all making up plausible scenarios to explain how and why, and here she was sitting in the middle of a field talking to a Pict. She must be dead or in a coma. She must have fallen and hit her head and was lying unconscious in that field where she'd scarfed her sandwich. It just figured her idea of Heaven would be some sort of historical fact-finding mission. And despite that she suspected this was all a dream, she tried to keep calm and answer his question. "All I know is my father was a Scot," she told him.

Across the fire, the old woman suddenly gave a decidedly disapproving, "Hurrumph!"

Callum paid the woman little mind. "How are your wrists?" he asked, changing the subject.

"Fine."

"I'm sorry for binding them, lass. 'Ye happened upon me whilst I was burying my Da."

"I know. I'm sorry too," she offered, and meant it.

The old woman suddenly bounded to her feet. "*Chan eil fhios càise*!" she announced, pointing at Annie, and left them, muttering. "*Dìt Scoti!*"

Alarmed by her outburst, Annie watched her march beyond the light of the fire, her painted body disappearing into the night.

"Dinna mind auld Morag," he said. "She's o' the mind no outlander is a good outlander, but the auld bat is harmless."

Annie wasn't so sure about that. "What did she say?"

"She said ye dinna know cheese,'" he disclosed with a grin. "That slice in your hand is as precious as your keek stane, and if ye were a Fidach in truth, ye'd know 'twas made by your own clanswomen for hundreds of years. But 'tis more like that her feelings are sore to see ye picking at it like a wee bird."

Callum seemed to be watching her curiously. "An' ye say ye lost your Da?"

"I was eight," she said, and hushed. The sense of loss was keen, even after all these years.

He stared at her—waiting for her to continue, she presumed. Despite his size and breadth, there was a gentleness about him and a comprehension in his gaze that Annie found effortless. Inexplicably, she found she trusted him. And in spite of the fact that she had never once discussed her parents' death with her own fiancé, she felt drawn toward sharing the pain of her loss with another human being. Unfortunately, how did one explain a drunk driver to a man who must know nothing of cars? "He was murdered," she said. And in a way it was true.

She knew he suspected the same about his own father though the circumstances were different. But they had something in common.

"What o' your minny?"

Annie smiled a little. "Immortal, remember?" That was true as well—at least in Annie's heart. Beneath her knees, the crystal glowed pink, catching her attention. So far, she hadn't said anything she didn't believe was true…

His gaze fell to the crystal she was keeping close. "Tell me aboot ye're keek stane, Annie Ross."

Annie reached down to pull the crystal close before he could think to touch it. "It's precious," she said, repeating the shopkeeper's claim.

"Aye, weel…if in fact it has the power to reveal all ye say it does, then mayhap it is," Callum relented.

"It can," Annie Ross persisted, guarding her crystal jealously between her lovely legs.

Magic or nay, it was clearly important to her, he reasoned. But she had another treasure hidden there that was far more valuable, and it had been far too long since a woman had hardened his cock so easily. She was lovely as a summer day, with a temper that fired his senses. And there was a look of keen intelligence in her eyes that stirred him far more deeply than any pair of diddies could manage. He had claimed she was daft, but she was far from it, he suspected, and he realized she was attracted to him as well. However, it would do her little good if he confessed to it now and endangered her life in the process.

Besides, if Biera returned and found the lass was lying…well, he didn't wish to grow attached to a woman who would end without a head.

He eyed the crystal, but he made no move to take it, sensing she was offering him a measure of trust. A mon could win more flies with honey than with vinegar, his minny used to say. The problem was that Callum could never determine what a mon might want with flies. On the other hand, he knew precisely what he wanted with the lass sitting before him now…

Answers…to begin with.

Nay, he didn't believe she was any faerie. She was a flesh and blood mortal, the same as him. Proof was in those rosy cheeks every time she dared to glance at the region of his lap. If he werna a disciplined man, he would have erected a small tent in his breacan the instant he sat down beside her.

He didn't believe she was a spy either, but god save her if she was. He'd take her head the same as any mon's. And if he didna do it himself, one of his kinsmen would…only then he would lose the fealty of his clan.

Succession was not absolute, nor was it decreed by patrimony. Among the old ones, it was the mother's blood that ruled. And fortunately for Callum—or mayhap not so fortunately—he had the advantage that both his parents' Pecht blood was true. These days, three generations removed from MacAilpín's treason, most men were Gaels by virtue of at least one parent's bloodline. It was a stain on their Pecht lineage, and their consortium had drawn together the last of his people whose blood was pure. None of these men or women who had been chosen for this mission were beholden to the Gaels, not by blood or fealty.

They sat quietly for a moment, listening to the persistent sound of hammers in the distance. Along the beach, his kinsmen were busy repairing the remains of an old crannog that had fallen into ruin. It made him heartsick to think that now the elders of all seven Pecht nations—Cat, Fidach, Ce, Fotla, Circinn, Fortriu and Fib—could fit into one small crannog. Alas, they were the last of the Painted Ones—those whom the Roman's had once called Pechts. Now they were the Guardians of *clach-na-cinneamhain*—the true Stone of Destiny, which was now hidden in the belly of the ben.

The lass picked up her crystal. The instant she touched it, the color changed.

"What does it mean when it turns green?"

She peered up at him in surprise, her eyes widening a bit.

CHAPTER SIX

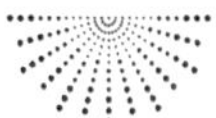

He could see it?

Still Annie didn't know how to respond, because she didn't really understand the crystal's properties. So far, she had only seen it turn that particular color in the hands of only two people...hers and the shopkeeper's so she took a wild guess. "It knows when it's in the hands of its keeper."

At her words, the crystal's ribbons shifted to a rosy hue.

It chooses ye, she recalled the shopkeeper's saying.

Callum seemed to be watching the crystal as well. Annie spared him but a glance, but her eyes returned to the crystal with sudden realization, "Of course," she said. "I am the keeper."

What else did the colors mean?

Truth, lies...and the destinies of men.

The old woman's words had been very specific, Annie believed. There were only two colors she had witnessed thus far, and all things might be determined through truth and lies. If green meant that a connection with the crystal had been forged, could red be truth instead of anger or passion? The crystal's rosy color intensified, even as she experienced the thought, and she marveled at it. It seemed to respond directly to all things connected to her.

Fae magic, the woman had claimed.

Could it be true?

What might be the color of a lie?

Lifting the crystal, she held it in front of her, peering into its depths. "I'm from another time and place," she enunciated clearly, without sparing a glance toward Callum, despite that the statement was as much for his benefit. The last of the green dissipated from the crystal so that it was permeated with threads of all shades of red.

Callum watched closely as her crystal seemed to react to her words. For an instant, he thought he detected a measure of surprise in her gaze, but she was looking at him now with something more akin to conviction.

"Are ye a spy for King Giric?" he asked directly.

She gave him her full attention then, and shook her head somberly, seeming to realize the import of his question. The stone's colors remained rosy and Callum thought she must be speaking truth. He decided to test her...and the crystal as well. "D' ye find me appealing, Annie Ross?"

Her gaze skidded toward his. "I...uh...haven't... thought about it," she stammered, and the crystal's color faded to a dirty brown, while her cheeks turned a lovely a shade of crimson.

The blood warmed in Callum's veins at the thought of her ardor—no matter that she denied it. God's teeth, even without the crystal's confirmation, he recognized desire in those clear green eyes—eyes that were far more knowing than any woman he had ever encountered.

Or any man for that matter.

For a moment, no words were spoken between them, and the breath of the world seemed to falter.

"D' ye wish to kiss me, lass?" he asked, no longer testing her. Nor did he any longer care whether his kinsmen were watching. Let them watch if they must. If she said yes, he would take her sweet bonny mouth right here and now.

"No!" she said too quickly. In her hands, the crystal darkened and then extinguished like a gutted torch.

Callum grinned at the sight of it. She was lying, and that pleased him inordinately.

It took the lass a full moment to realize her stone had betrayed her, and once she did, he laughed low. "Seems your keek stane does indeed reveal truth and lies, Annie Ross. I'll be watching what ye say from here forth." And then, having imparted as much, he stood. "I dinna wish to kiss ye either," he lied. "An' I dinna like ye at all," he declared before walking away—before she could note the darkened color of her keek stane.

As he made his way back to the crannog, he found himself grinning stupidly, wishing Biera would hurry back to declare the lass innocent, because if it was the last thing Callum did, he intended to convince Annie Ross to remain here with him in the vale, to bear his bairns and warm his bed. With the right person in his arms, not even the cold could diminish his spirit.

Brude was right: Callum *was* far more motivated to finish the crannog now, and it was because of Annie Ross. If he had to work until the torches gutted tonight, he vowed not to stop until he had a private place to woo the woman he intended to make his bride.

And yet…no one else seemed to have noted the changing colors of her stone, so while he believed her, he realized the others might not, so until Biera returned, he must keep the lass at bay…a task that might not prove so simple if she continued to look at him that way—with that incredible look of longing that made him want to taste the nectar of her body.

Aye, he wanted her, but for now, it was enough to know that wherever she had come from—faerie or nay—the gods had surely sent her to settle his restless heart.

"D' ye wish to kiss me, lass?"

Those sensual lips were branded in Annie's memory. To emphasize her lie, the Winter Stone remained dark—no longer red, green or milky white.

"D' ye wish to kiss me?"

No.

Yes.

The crystal's color brightened suddenly, revealing shards of pink.

Damn it.

She *did* want to kiss him. It was true. The way he had looked at her set her heart to racing, even now that he was nowhere near. He wasn't immune to her either, despite his claims to the contrary. She only wished she had known how to use the crystal better, so she could have made a liar out of him as he had done to her.

Bloody hell, he'd used her own stone against her.

But why was it that only the two of them could see its colors, aside from the shopkeeper? Annie wondered.

Curled beneath her cheap poncho, she tried to make herself as small as she was able so she might better fit beneath the fringed garment. It was pointless. It was cold and she was restless. Once the sun went down, the temperature plummeted and her teeth might have begun to chatter except that the object of her newest obsession appeared long enough to dump a heavy woolen cloak over her. He gave her a wink—as though they were long-time allies—and then walked away.

"Wait!" Annie grabbed her stone, eager for an opportunity to redeem herself. "Wait!" she called after him, but he ignored her, marching deliberately away, without looking back, his shoulders shaking with what she suspected was mirth.

He was toying with her.

Did he realize what he had done to her?

Damn him.

Frustrated, Annie turned, giving grumpy Morag her back.

Embraced by Callum's cloak, she realized how thin and poorly made her modern poncho was and she was heartily grateful for Callum's thoughtful gesture…except that now…she could smell him on her covers—the scent of man, sun and sweat. It was entirely disturbing and it sent her thoughts skittering to places they shouldn't wander. Nor could she stop imagining him working out there…somewhere…bare-assed. She stared into the Winter Stone, admitting the truth—she wanted him—and the rosy color of the stone heightened.

"Okay, yes," she confessed to the stubborn rock. "Yes, damn it! I do!"

Over by the fire Morag muttered something crossly beneath her breath and continued to stoke the flames. Thankfully, after awhile, one of the men came to take her place. The two exchanged words Annie couldn't quite make out and then she was alone again with a new guard—thankfully, whose temperament wasn't half so grim. But if she had thought Callum a tall man, this guy loomed over her like a lumbering pine. He sat—or more like, folded like an accordion to his knees. "'*S thoigh le Callum Annie às Ross,*" he said with a lopsided grin.

Annie couldn't be certain, but she thought he had uttered some third-grade proclamation, something like, "Callum likes Annie Ross."

She smirked. It gave her a curious sense of satisfaction to know that someone else had noticed as well, even if Callum refused to confess it. Seriously, if the situation wasn't so…bizarre…she might have laughed. What in God's name was she supposed to say to that? Except that, apparently, she kind of liked Callum back. She smiled tentatively at the man, and he rewarded her with his flask, handing it over after taking another hefty chug.

Thirsty, tired, cold and grateful for his show of kindness, Annie didn't hesitate. She greedily accepted the flask and took a quick drink.

Liquid fire poured down her throat and she swallowed as she choked. She thought it might be whisky, but she couldn't be sure. It tasted more like gasoline. Good lord! She might have realized water wasn't a thing here—they probably didn't know how to boil yet, she thought sardonically. And despite her sour face, her new companion laughed amiably. "*Is ainm dhomh Dunneld,*" he said, offering up his name.

For a moment, Annie could barely speak past the burn in her throat. She handed the flask back, and said, "Good to meet you, Dunneld."

He took another turn with the flask, putting the homemade whisky down as easily as though it were milk. "Ye as well, lass." His grin widened. "If ye ask me," he proffered, "ye're a gift from the gods, fae or no'." He nodded when she furrowed her brow. "Until ye appeared, Callum was all set to go. Puir lad. He dinna take his da's passing well. In truth, he's never been quite convinced of…our…" He averted his gaze suddenly, looking a bit disconcerted as he finished, "mission." But then he peered back at her, grinning once more, and he shook his head with what appeared to be genuine wonder. "Ye'd best be getting' yourself some rest," he advised with a wink, and chased his warning with another swig of whisky. "Ye're just the thing tae keep the chief settled, I warrant."

Annie blushed. It probably wouldn't do much good to assure the man that she didn't intend to remain here all that long. Once her curiosity was appeased over the Stone of Destiny, she'd be applying herself twenty-four-seven to finding a way back home—no matter how much Callum invaded her thoughts.

Why?

The question popped into her head, like a disembodied voice, unsettling her.

She lay back on her elbow against the ground, pulling the cloak up nearly to her chin. These people had not harmed her, despite that they had questioned her motives. So why not explore whatever this was she was feeling? What was there to get back to anyway?

Everything, she mentally replied. *Everything*. Then again, *nothing.*

That thought made her glum.

"Come near the fire, Annie Ross," Dunneld dc manded, not unkindly. "The night's cauld."

"Thank you." Annie said.

"'S e do bheatha." You're welcome.

Annie considered the man sitting in front her—and Callum as well—both far more polite than most guys she knew. And for a time, she lay watching him draw pensively with his stick in the ash, wondering who would miss her if she didn't return home. Maybe Kate? She only saw her cousin once every year or so. She did have friends, but everyone was busy with their own lives, raising babies and trying to crash glass ceilings. Annie had always felt a bit like a fish out of water—something she was, inconceivably, not feeling at the moment. She ought to be questioning why. "Where exactly are we, Dunneld?"

The giant's brows collided. "Ach, now, ye walked here w' ye're ain two legs. How is it ye dinna know where ye be?"

Faced with such a common sense question, and having absolutely no answer, Annie furrowed her brow. "I don't know." Everything she'd thought she'd known was upside down.

The night was dark, but the firelight cast a warm glow over Dunneld's face, highlighting the red in his beard. He took another swig from his flask, nodding. And he must have decided he believed her, because he waved a hand over the entire expanse and said, "'Tis a sacred vale...MacAilpín himself brought together seven kings here to sup as friends." His voice took on a somber tone. "Black Tolargg, Drust, all of them... slaughtered like lambs upon an altar."

He tossed his stick into the fire and watched it burn. Intense sadness entered his eyes, revealed by the flickering of the flames. Lost in thoughts she could not glean, he drank more of his whisky, his tongue loosening a bit as he continued. He said the words as though he had held them in far too long. "The bastard said his minny was a Pecht," he recounted bitterly. "Though he was naught but a wolf in sheep's clothing—a faithless Gael..."

"Who?"

"MacAilpín—the bastard."

Annie suddenly remembered Callum's words:... *there's no' a one of us who would benefit by siding with the sons of MacAilpín.* Her heart tripped a little. The possibility that she might be sharing the same air as the Father of Scotland made her feel lightheaded, but apparently neither Dunneld nor Callum held him in high regard. "Where is he now?" she asked, and held her breath for his answer.

"Who?"

"Kenneth MacAilpín."

He gave her an incredulous look. "Ach! *Dead* now—for twenty years or more!"

Disappointment sidled through her. "Oh. I didn't realize."

He arched a brow. "Mayhap then ye be a faerie, in truth, because I dinna ken how any mon or woman wadna know. That liar died with a lump in his throat the size o' my fist—cursed by the gods, yet buried in Iona as befits a saint. 'Tis true enough only his Gael brothers mourn him now for my kin willna so easily forget 'twas Kenneth MacAilpín who murdered our sires…"

"Twenty years?" Annie sighed with disappointment. But there was still the stone…and she had lived her entire academic life for this question, so she had to know. "What about the stone…the one you brought from Scone?"

Momentarily caught off guard by the question, Dunneld peered up at her through dark lashes. "Seems I've said too much already, Annie Ross. Dinna fash yersel' o'er it. Get some rest now afore auld Morag returns an' ye find yersel' squirming beneath *an droch-shùil!*" *The evil eye.*

Annie laughed softly. She lay her head back upon the ground and peered up at the black sky, listening to the endless echo of hammers in the distance.

Until ye appeared, Callum was all set to go…

Callum likes Annie Ross.

Yes, he did and she was going to prove it, she vowed—if it was the last thing she did before she left here. A feeling like butterflies flittered somewhere down deep in her belly, and her heart tripped again. If she was dead, in fact...or dreaming...if this was heaven...at least God had gotten her version of heaven exactly right—surrounded by the history she loved...

Unconsciously pulling Callum's cloak to her nostrils, Annie breathed deeply of his male scent and studied the night sky. These were all the same stars—exactly where they belonged. Even the North Star, bright as it was, was in plain sight. If she was dreaming...then she was doing it in amazing detail. High above, stars twinkled like faerie dust, lulling her into closing her eyes. And somehow she fell into a deep, weary sleep, despite a growing sense of anticipation she attributed to the fantastic possibility of setting eyes upon the Stone of Destiny...but it was much, much more than that, she knew.

She didn't stir at the changing of her guard.

CHAPTER SEVEN

Higher on the hill, guards changed there as well.

The caves, naturally formed and full of mist, descended deep into the bowels of the ben. That's where they had vaulted the stone. But this was as close as any need come, for the cold mist was enough to put an ague in the bones. There was no other way in, so the guards remained outside, guarding from without. Voices carried so they fell into whispers—one an elder, one not. It so happened the two had received the same rotation this evening.

"If she's a spy, she wasna sent here by Giric," the elder declared.

"How can ye know?"

The elder shrugged. Using his dirk to pare off an annoying hang of flesh at his thumb, he pricked a bit of his own blood, and then swiped it upon his breacan. "Let us simply say I was kept in confidence until we left Scone."

"Tell me then, if Giric realizes the stone missing, why has he no' raised alarm and stormed the vale?"

The elder eyed the man seated upon his rump and re-sheathed his blade. "Of course, they have no idea where we have taken the stone—how could they? No one has left this god-forsaken vale since the day we arrived—except Biera, the auld bitch."

"Ye shouldna speak of her that way. She has the ear of the gods, they say."

"Chan eil agad ach a' bhreug!" Nothing but lies! "She's but an old crone," the elder maintained. "If'n ye ask me, she's off to drink the summer away—as we should be doing. She's no' Cailleach Bheur!"

The storm that had threatened earlier had fled entirely. The night sky was clear without a breath of wind, but from within the caverns, a cold mist rolled out, settling over the hillside.

"Anyhow," the elder continued. "Giric wadna want anyone to know his coronation was no' consecrated—especially now that MacAilpín's grandsons have both fled Scotia."

As far as the elder was concerned, they had but three choices now. Only one was palatable. One would have them siding with Giric, the usurper, who was even now prepared to wed one of their blood and realign the royal houses. Another would see the noble houses of Pechtland rot, alone, in this vale, along with that accursed Destiny Stone, while the new kingdom of Scotia set its own path, giving its kingship to the sons and daughters of Gaels. And then, of course, they could return the stone publicly, for which they would all likely hang. And, of course, Giric might as well, and the line of succession would return to men who cared not a wit about the Pechts. At least Giric mac Dúngail was willing to wed the elder's daughter, but no one else knew that, save the man at his feet. But just in case he thought to change his mind, the elder reminded, "Giric will pay in gold if we return the stone—with positions in his court. It canna be worse than this—a cauld, hard ground in the middle of the Mounth, with the ides of winter on the way."

And then for a time, both fell silent, staring into the starry night.

When all was said and done, hiding away the Stone of Destiny to keep those Gael bastards from slitting each others' throats was not their duty. Not even Callum was convinced of it. The elder had nearly had him cajoled to go back...nearly. And then *that woman* had arrived...

"We have failed to persuade him," the man at his feet said soberly, as though reading his thoughts.

"Nay—*you* have failed," the elder countered. "A fact which aggrieves me to no end, for it forced my hand."

The man nodded, eyes shadowed. "At least Finn died quickly. Poor bastard."

"Poor bastard? He always had aught he desired—whenever he desired. Did he not woo everyone to this end with nary more than a drunkard's tale? Nay, I dinna feel an ounce of regret for what is done. Finn could ha' taken his place at Giric's side simply for the asking, yet he appointed himself the guardian of the Stone instead. All men must live by their choices. He but died for his."

"Because he believed the stone to be cursed."

"Bollocks!" The elder exclaimed. "That stone is naught more than a worthless slab some bampot toted here on his back from Erin. We are defeated if we remain in this vale, dinna forget it."

Both men fell into silence again.

The elder determined they must not fail. Not at any cost. There was too much to lose. He could not allow the man to waver, but just in case, he had already begun to whisper in Angus's ear. Like Fergus, Angus was an elder, much respected by his clan.

"I thought mayhap Callum suspected...when he

questioned what any might have to gain by siding with the sons of MacAilpín..."

The elder gave him a sideways glance. "Of course he asks the wrong question and dismisses Giric out of hand."

"How many know why Máel remained in Scone?"

"None," the elder reassured. "Why would anyone question a daughter's right to remain with her ailing minny?"

The man nodded. "So now Callum has returned to repairing the crannog."

"Fool."

Silence. "Should we kill the lass?"

The elder heard hesitation in the man's voice. He scoffed. "Lest ye believe she's a fae and ye're afeared to anger the gods? But nay, I'll do better," he assured with a slow grin. "I'll let Callum do it for us...then, once he leaves the vale, our task will go all the easier, for although he doesna realize as yet, he is the one who keeps the others constant. Once he leaves, 'twill be a simple matter to convince them that returning the stone is to our greatest advantage."

"But what if killing the lass isna enough?"

The elder shrugged. He thought about it only a moment, then suggested, "Then we must kill Callum as well."

HALF EXPECTING to find it had all been a dream, Annie's lashes fluttered open to find she was lying beside Callum upon a pallet in a strange room. On the floor. Covered by tartans. Below the floorboards, she heard the distinct sound of sloshing water.

She had slept so soundly that she had only a vague memory of him carrying her here, snuggling her against his warm chest, walking gently, so as not to wake her.

She smiled knowingly. Right, so he wasn't attracted to her and he didn't like her?

She tried to rise, but he must have been awake, because his arm shot out to keep her next to him. His morning voice was gruff. "Ye're here for ye're protection," he explained, despite that she didn't ask.

"Really?" Absurdly, she welcomed the weight of his muscular arm across her breasts, and she stretched, pressing them into his arm, taunting him. "Not even a wee bit because you want me?"

"Nay," he answered, without hesitation.

Feeling smug at the thought of checking her Winter Stone now, Annie pushed his arm aside and sought her crystal, intending to show it to him. "Oh, no!" she exclaimed, realizing it was no longer with her. "Where is it?"

She sat straight up, searching the empty room. There was not a stitch of wall covering or furniture here. The room was bare and her Winter Stone was gone. He merely shifted to look at her, pulling the cloak back so she could clearly see he didn't have her crystal. "Haud yer wheesht, lass. Your keek stane is safe."

It was only then she realized he was completely bare beside her and her natural reaction was to scramble out of the pallet, though her alarm was quickly tempered by the fact that he hadn't bothered to touch her all night long. And very quick on the heels of that realization was a keen sense of disappointment—which made about zero sense.

He lifted a brow. "Ach, lass, ye'd think ye'd ne'er seen a mon's *bod* before."

"A what?"

His lips curved entirely too roguishly. "That thing

you're ogling now as though it were a one-eyed demon."

Annie's cheeks heated. "Well!" she exclaimed. "I've never seen *yours*!" And she wished she hadn't even now, because there it was—well, hardly…hard. He was without a doubt the most well endowed man she had ever seen without pants, but he wasn't the least bit aroused.

Maybe he really wasn't attracted to her? She wasn't Kate, after all…but she wasn't chopped liver either. Maybe her cousin was right and she did need a makeover?

"Are ye done yet?" he asked with a conspicuous note of laughter in his voice. "And yet if it please ye…take a closer look, and mayhap I'll change my mind."

Annie blinked away the confusion from her mind. She stood, brushing off her poncho, and finally pulled off the price tag, crushing it in her fist. "Where's my stone?" she demanded.

He was still grinning, and the sight of his smile was maddening. She could see the way he was looking at her and she was certain he was attracted to her, no matter what he claimed.

She wanted her crystal back!

"Ye blush well for a faerie," he said, ignoring her question. "Di' ye no' say so…I would think ye were flesh and blood same as me."

"Why wouldn't a faerie blush?" she challenged.

Callum's grin widened at the question.

She was a true Highlander—spirited and bold, no matter where she had come from. Aye, she would fit in very well with the women of his clan—all of whom would as soon box a mon's ears as to bow down before him.

"If you're thinking of ravaging me, don't," she warned. "I know karate."

Callum chuckled. He didn't move from where he lay, though he did cover himself to give her eyes respite. "I dinna know what karate is," he assured her, "but rest ye well, lass, for I dinna have ravaging in mind. Why the hell would ye say such a thing?"

She narrowed her green eyes at him. "Why else would you sleep like *that* in the middle of winter?" she demanded, her tone full of censure. "You *are* attracted to me." she persisted, "Why don't you admit it!"

Callum screwed his face at her. "Winter? Nay, lass, 'tis summer yet, and I slept this way..." He rose from the pallet, retrieving his breacan. "... because ye were shivering like a willow and I meant tae keep ye warm." He lifted a brow. "Ye dinna show much appreciation, and yet ye're welcome nonetheless."

"Oh," she said with far less sass, and then she had the good graces to look disconcerted and mayhap a little chastened. "In that case...thank you...I guess." But her lovely face screwed with what he read as disappointment.

Callum's shoulders shook again with mirth. She stood before him, looking for all the world like a wildling, ready to flee, but her eyes begged him to know her as a man would know a woman. He wrapped his breacan about himself, covering his nakedness so she might finally look at him straight in the face—not out of the corner of her eyes—for he had the sudden yen to spy the color of those eyes: green rimmed by the color of aged *uisge*.

Unlike Callum, she had slept fully dressed. And despite his claims to the contrary, aye, the sight of her lovely bare legs tested his resolve.

If the gods be willing, he fully intended to bed the lass, but she would be the one to ask. He'd make her beg, in fact, and then he would hold her by his side forevermore, guarding her jealously, for after seeing her in the morning light, with her lovely black hair, mussed from sleep, and those sweet rosy cheeks, he knew she would make him the envy of every man. But inasmuch as she seemed intrigued by his *bod*, he sensed it would take far more than the *gift* he was blessed with to truly win her heart and make her stay here with him in the vale. Nay, lust would not be enough—not for him either—for he craved something more—something that had eluded him with all the women of seven clans.

But right now, he needed to know for certain what had brought her to this vale and he intended to set a test for her. For her sake, he hoped she'd pass. "I have something I wish to show ye," he said with a slow grin, sensing he knew how to tempt the winsome lass. Her gaze slid toward his groin and he laughed, and reassured, "Nay, lass, not *that*."

CHAPTER EIGHT

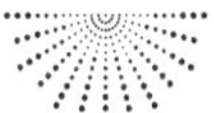

Annie's cheeks were still burning as Callum led her out of the crannog—a cone shaped dwelling that sat out on the lake. She had visited one a few years back out on Loch Tay. Only this one was quite some larger, built with smaller dens encircling a big hall. It was clear that the structure had seen better days, but they were busy making repairs. Already this morning the men were at work, hauling in timber, and now that they had abandoned the chieftain's quarters, the noise level increased.

A single door led out to a narrow pier that stretched out toward the shore. Once off the pier, Callum took her by the hand. Stunned by the gesture, Annie allowed it, wondering when the last time was that she'd held a man's hand.

While her thoughts were entirely pre-occupied with the strange way Callum made her feel, he led her across the vale and up a hill, apparently not caring that his kinsmen were all watching. They knew he liked her, and his actions only illustrated that fact—if only she could get him to admit it. "I really, *really* need my Winter Stone," she fretted.

"Dinna fash yerself, lass."

Annie had never really considered herself obsessive in nature, but clearly she was, because she seemed to have a one-track mind where Callum was concerned. "Where I come from, men only hold a woman's hand if they *like* them."

"In that place ye say you're from?" he asked without looking at her. "What is it? Merica?"

"*A*-merica," Annie replied. And then she brooded, because he simply refused to confess. She couldn't possibly be the only one experiencing these feelings? She had half a mind to throw herself at him and kiss him right here in the field. She combed her hair with her fingers and tried to find the nerve.

In the bright light of day, the valley was gorgeous. Unsullied. The grass was still green and the sky was bluer than Annie had ever seen it. Yesterday's storm had never come to fruition, but it didn't appear this valley lacked for water. In fact, it was as rich and verdant as she'd ever seen it.

She followed Callum up the hillside to an opening in a cave, where two surly men sat guarding the entrance. A sudden frisson of excitement flew through her, finally displacing her wayward thoughts. She had come here searching for a cave, and here one was…

She turned to appraise the area, trying to calculate where she was.

"Ye recall my uncle Brude?" Callum proffered, and the man, with his two-pronged beard, merely scowled at her. Callum gestured to the other, seated on his rump. "Angus," he said, introducing them.

Angus tipped his head, and cast a narrow-eyed glance at Brude. The two shared a look of surprise as Callum invited her within the cave. Neither voiced a complaint, however, and Annie surmised neither dared, despite his uncle's dissention last night.

"Where are we going?" she asked at his back, though

she was beginning to sense she already knew, and her heart was pounding like a drum against her ribs. And for the first time since she'd arrived here, it had nothing to do with the man leading her through the maze of caves.

Callum peered back at her, flashing perfect white teeth in the darkness of the cave—a smile any dentist would love. "I'm going to show ye what ye came to see..."

CHAPTER NINE

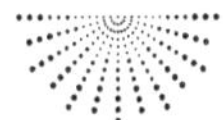

The Stone of Destiny.

Lia Fail, as it was hailed by the Irish.

Callum's people called it *Clach-na-cinneamhain.*

Whatever it's name, there it sat upon an altar made of rough hewn stone in the center of the deepest cave, with mist rising from unseen places.

Even having braced herself for the sight of it, Annie wasn't fully prepared.

It didn't glow with some holy light. It didn't even look holy. It was just a big dark lump of volcanic rock...and yet...it was magnificent. Drawn to it like a magnet to metal, Annie bolted across the room. Thankfully, Callum didn't hold her back.

The stone, much darker than the one that sat beneath the chair in Westminster Abbey for seven hundred years, was smooth on top, polished by the years. She knew in every way that it was different because she had taken a thousand photos of that other one with her missing camera. And as she had suspected, this one wasn't made of sandstone. It was made of what appeared to be basalt. Unlike the one commonly held as the Stone of Scone, it had no handles on either side, but there were holes where handles might have once been.

Clearly, it wasn't an easy object to tote around. Seeing it up close, she knew beyond a shadow of doubt that the stone returned to Edinburgh in 1996 was a fake.

This one bore an intricately carved metal plaque. Annie ran her fingers over the etched letters, worn with age, but clearly visible.

Unless the fates be faulty grown
And prophet's voice be vain
Where'er is found this sacred stone
The blood of Alba reigns.

Her throat was suddenly thick, and she found it difficult to swallow.

Here it is, daddy. Here it is!

Now this was a stone to last the ages! That other sandstone block that had been seized by Edward had broken at least once when it was stolen from Westminster. But that's just the sort of thing that had kept Annie so intrigued by this puzzle—that the widely accepted answers were not the ones that made sense.

But this...*this* made sense—*this* had *always* made sense—that the stone would have been hidden somewhere in the hillside. She had been so certain of it, despite having no proof. And now she knew precisely where it was.

The moment was so incredibly breathtaking Annie only belatedly realized her crystal was glowing softly in the corner—a ghostly green light.

Her ticket home.

If she found her way home using the crystal...would the Stone of Destiny be right here? She didn't recall this cave from her walkabouts. Had they hidden the entrance somehow? Had it collapsed over time? She ran her fingers over the top of the smooth stone, where it had worn to a soft sheen, and she peered up at Callum, recalling him only then. That's how entranced she was by this discovery...for an instant the stone had eclipsed the one man in her life that she had been drawn to at first sight.

It was true. She had never felt quite such an electric attraction with anyone. Nor ever so at ease in someone's presence. Something was different with Callum... very different.

She blinked at him, seeing him with whole new eyes. For all that he looked like a barbarian, he was the most civilized man she had ever known. He was letting her enjoy this moment, somehow sensing how momentous it was for her. Never once had Paul allowed himself to fall second place to anything she cared about. She didn't think then, merely acted. She turned, celebrating the moment, and threw her arms around Callum's neck, kissing him soundly—not to prove anything, but just because. Because she wanted to kiss this man as much as she had wanted to find the Stone of Destiny.

He made some startled sound, then relaxed in her embrace, automatically wrapping his arms about her waist, and Annie reveled in the strength of them.

And then the world held its breath as their lips melted together into a searing kiss...the most passionate, heartfelt, knee-weakening kiss of Annie's life. In that heady instant she no longer needed the Winter Stone to verify what she already knew...his body hardened between them, pressing against her, and all rational thought extinguished at the feel of it. Without thinking, only feeling, her hand slid between them, finding all the evidence she needed.

"You want me," she said softly, smirking, and the Winter Stone burned brighter in the corner, its color warming the room in shades of pink.

"Ach, God," Callum protested, but the feel of her hand along his shaft evaporated his resolve. To hell with waiting for Biera. To hell with trials and restless kinsmen. If any man dared to touch this woman, he'd rip out his heart with his own hands.

If he needed proof that Annie was flesh and blood, he had it now, for her skin set fire to his hands and his lips. "Aye," he told her gruffly. "I want ye, lass." And then he lifted her up on the stone table, his body trembling with a desire he had never experienced with any woman in all his nearly thirty years.

For all his attempts to deny her—and himself—his ardor spun into reality like a tempest, filling his veins with liquid fire.

Reaching between them, he sought her wetness and was thwarted by her tiny red breeches. For an instant, he considered gently removing them, but they were a senseless garment anyway and—gah!—they were in his way. His hands trembled as he ripped the delicate lace, his brain fogged with desire. He tossed them onto the floor as she squirmed against his belly, seeking the part of him that was harder now than the bloody stone. Instead of complaining, she moaned softly into the back of his throat and spread her legs like a beautiful flower.

"Oh, yes," Annie whispered, and instinctively wrapped her legs around Callum's hips, anchoring herself with his body, hardly aware of thought, only feeling. Somewhere in the back of her head she winced over the thought of where he would take her—right here on the Stone of Destiny. But she was powerless to stop this now. Her skin was on fire, her breasts ached to be free, the muscles of her legs tensed and her body throbbed to have him inside—literally throbbed, she marveled, as she spread her legs as far as they would go, willing him to come inside her.

He kissed her senseless, never breaking the contact of their lips, and Annie's desire spiraled out of control. The sight of her torn, red, lace panties on the floor only made her want him more. It was further proof of his desire though his hands remained gentle.

She wanted more.

His fingers didn't disappoint her. He pressed one inside her body, groaning as he found her wet to the touch. Annie moaned too in response, sliding down to give him better access. But his fingers weren't enough. She wanted more. She wanted *everything* he had shown her this morning and she wanted it *now*. Her heart beat faster, the sound of it like thunder in her ears.

Then suddenly it was there, his skin hot against hers, pressing hard, and Annie cried out and slid down over his shaft, reveling in the delicious way it stretched her body as she took him inside.

She sighed with satisfaction and deepened the kiss, mimicking with her tongue exactly how she wanted him to move inside her. She felt so naughty, but oh, so good.

It happened so fast. And for once in her life she didn't care about anyone but the two hearts beating in this room. The Winter Stone glowed brightly in the corner and a cold mist rose from their feet, intensifying the heat of Callum's hands. Annie felt as though she were on fire.

She had no idea how she'd come to be here, but suddenly it felt more like home than anywhere else had ever felt.

They made love against the stone, and she couldn't have cared less that her back was chafing against the rock. His arms embraced her as he thrust inside her, filling her completely and withdrawing, giving her the most intense pleasure she had ever known.

By all the gods, Callum couldn't have stopped himself if he had tried. But he didn't. Wouldn't. It had been far too long since he had craved a woman's body so desperately.

She wasn't the least bit timid, matching his desire and surpassing it tenfold. She was a goddess, his faerie princess, desire incarnate.... He reveled in her body and her passion, groaning with pleasure when she filled his mouth with her soft coos of release. And then instead of growing timid with the return of rational thought, she merely grinned at him, and whispered, her tone filled with satisfaction, "I knew it," she said. "You *do* like me."

Her Winter Stone lit the entire grotto with a fiery glow that matched his ardor, and he found his release instantly, filling her body with a powerful burst of seed. And in that heady moment, Callum knew he believed in faeries after all, for there was naught that could explain what had passed between them here but to describe it as magic. Forever more, that ridge whereupon he had discovered her would be known as the faerie glen.

"So ye did, lass," he whispered with a deeper sense of satisfaction than he'd ever felt. "So ye did. And hereto, I pledge ye my troth...if ye will have me, Annie Ross."

CHAPTER TEN

Startled by his words, Annie lay back upon the Stone of Destiny.

Talk about fear of commitment—he apparently had none at all. How far they had come…when men no longer saw this act as a bond.

He let her go, but his hands sought and cupped her breasts, gently, as only a lover would. His hands continued to worship her body, even once they were done, and he continued to move inside her, as though to caress her from within.

"I will cherish and protect you always," he swore. "And I will be true, for I dinna mean to sire bairns who will go through life without a Da."

Reality swept into the cave, with a gust of cold mist, but Annie didn't move. She hadn't even considered that. *Damn.*

She couldn't stay. Now more than ever she needed to go back…to prove herself to the scientific community.

What had she done?

He might be everything she had ever fantasized about in a man, but this was not her world. She had clearly been sent here to find the stone so she could reveal it to a doubting-Thomas world.

Her hand fanned out over the stone she was lying upon. "Why is it here?" she asked, changing the subject, because now she was confused.

"We brought it here."

"Why?"

Callum weighed his answer.

There was something about the look in her eyes that compelled him to speak the truth. "The stone is cursed," he said. "We hid it for the good of men."

She turned her cheek against the cold, hard stone, caressing it with her soft face in a manner that made him envious. From the instant he had first laid eyes upon her, she had been honest with him. The stone was what she had sought. Now he prayed to the gods—old and new—that she would not betray him with the knowledge he had given her. He wanted to trust her, but he surely didn't intend to allow her to leave here now with her precious Winter Stone. He wasn't so naive as to allow her to see the Destiny Stone and then set her free with the one possession she seemed to value above all.

And yet...he dared to hope...

Sensing she wanted to hear more, and feeling a need to re-affirm their mission for himself, he told her. "*Clach-na-cinneamhain* belonged to the Gaels first. 'Twas their holy relic, brought to us from Erin. Once our nations were joined with MacAilpín upon the throne, the Destiny Stone was blessed by one of our priestesses so that any chief who sits upon it and wields the sword of the *Righ Art*—the consecrated blade of the High King and Chief of Chiefs—will rule undivided lands. Our councils chose a new name for a new nation—a name neither Gael nor Pecht. And for a time there was peace..."

"Then what?" she asked, her green eyes luminous by the light of her keek stane, which glowed far brighter than a simple rock should. Only Biera had knowledge of such things.

"Then…MacAilpín murdered the sons of seven nations in order to secure his right to his precious throne. He broke our blood truce. Now the stone that was meant to bring unity must curse any mon who sits upon it without right to war against his kin. *Clach-na-cinneamhain* is no longer a blessing to men. To leave it in their hands is to ensure Scotia's rivers always run red."

She was quiet for a time, and as she lay there, the light from her Winter Stone waned…

"What if it's not the stone's fault?" she asked. "What if it's simply…destiny?"

Annie turned her gaze to his face, her thoughts reeling.

How much should she tell him?

Should she say that even without the stone, the sons of Scotland would continue to war against one another…until finally they were defeated? From history, she knew the grandsons of Kenneth MacAilpín would return from Ireland, more Gaels than Picts, and they would defeat the usurper Giric and take back the Scottish throne. However, once those boys returned, the legacy of Callum's people would come to an abrupt end. No matter what they did with this stone, brother would continue to kill brother and the Picts would soon be gone…nothing left but a memory.

The man she was talking to was literally the last of his kind…

She took a deep breath and turned away, wanting to know more about Callum…wanting to know where, precisely, these people were fated to go…once she was gone.

The cave went completely dark. Her Winter Stone was no longer illuminating the grotto, and Callum must have sensed her withdrawal, because he quietly broke their union, repaired her dress, and then said, "Your keek stane will be safe here…until we decide what to do w' ye."

Annie's gaze snapped up to meet his. She sat up, pulling down her skirt. "What to do with me? What do you mean?"

He nodded soberly, his expression grim though she could barely see him through the shadows now. A single torch sat within a brace on the far wall, but it left his face in shadows. "Aye. Ye'll have a proper trial once Biera returns." His voice was no longer warm. "Until then, ye'll have free reign to do as ye will. But take heed, lass…if ye leave the vale, an' we dinna take your head for it, I will destroy your keek stane, make no mistake."

So much for whatever sense of closeness she had felt.

His mood changed as abruptly as her Winter Stone—and she sucked in a breath as she realized why. She tried to recall what she'd said, but couldn't pinpoint the instant during which the stone had grown dark and cold.

She wasn't too worried about losing her head, despite that there wasn't any chance she would leave without the Winter Stone. However, she was very concerned about the idea that her fate was in the hands of someone she had never met. "Who is this Biera?"

"Our priestess…the one who led us here…the one who cursed the Destiny Stone. My father trusted her counsel without fail."

"And you don't?"

"I believe in what I see," he told her. "Nothing more."

But Annie didn't any longer—and maybe she never had. Because if that were true she would never have gone searching for the Stone of Destiny. She would never have found hope in an obscure newspaper article, or stubbornly set out into the hillside all on her own, because while all those things made perfect sense to Annie, they were hardly things that made sense to anyone else. Still she didn't know where to go from here…

She turned to peer at the crystal that was no longer radiating in the corner and then looked up at Callum, advising him, "Sometimes, Callum, you've got to go on faith."

CHAPTER ELEVEN

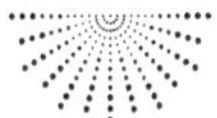

Following her own advice, as the days passed, Annie held onto faith that she could find a way home. However, stuck for the time being, she made the most of it, learning as much about these people and their customs as they would allow. To Annie they seemed little like the accounts from Bede and his contemporaries. But, alas, history wasn't objective. She found these people to be gentle and in tune with nature, but protective of themselves and their kin, and clearly ready to do battle for the things they believed in. As with any society there were cliques, and she later realized why they seemed to be so pronounced here. These were the last remaining of seven Pict tribes. The elders that had gathered around the fire on her first night in the vale were their representatives. It also explained why some of them wore different animal figures painted upon their bodies. She thought it might be a sort of family association—the wolf being Callum's association.

Brude also sported a wolf, while all of the other elders that night had worn different animals, one for each tribe. Later, she learned why there had been two wearing the wolf insignia that night around the fire:

Apparently, Callum's tribe was torn between giving the leadership of his clan to Finn's brother Brude and Callum, the son. For her sake, she hoped Callum won the honor, and apparently this was also something Biera was supposed to decide...along with Annie's fate.

Callum assured her that the old priestess would be fair and that her heart was true, but Annie needed to find a way to leave *long* before she arrived. So while she took mental notes about everything she saw, she also set her mind to devising a plan to get her crystal back.

There must be a way.

To that end, Dunneld was her greatest ally, even though he didn't realize it. Callum had assigned the braw warrior to look after her, and with him at her side she had free reign over the entire vale. He went about the task amiably, if a little distractedly, following Annie around like a curious puppy. He explained things when she asked, but more often, he would become distracted by his own shadow. If she had ever seen a textbook case for ADHD, he was it.

Once she caught him staring at her breasts as he was showing her the new storehouse. But as it turned out, it wasn't her breasts he was ogling. His gaze had been drawn to the safety pin she had hooked on her blouse. So she took it off and gave it to him and he walked around staring at the shiny metallic invention as though it were the greatest puzzle. Callum too had been curious over things like zippers and socks. She couldn't imagine what he might think about televisions or airplanes.

"Ow!" Dunneld exclaimed, every so often, and Annie smiled to herself, knowing why. The pin wasn't one of those flimsy copper safety pins. It was new and tight and she had pricked her own finger while trying to get it pinned the first time.

That day she learned the crannog was an old structure they were rebuilding, while all of the other buildings were being constructed from the ground up. They had hauled the timber from the old forests, only as much as they required.

While Dunneld was pre-occupied with her pin, Annie inspected the hillside, searching for fissures in the mountain that might hint at another access into the caverns. So far, nothing was apparent, and hoping to get closer, she dragged Dunneld up the hillside—still fidgeting with her pin—and talked him into escorting her into the outermost cave. But that's as far as he was willing to go. He refused to take her deeper, and stubbornly planted himself between Annie and the rope ladder that led down into the grotto. But even from there, Annie could *feel* her crystal calling to her—a sort of energy that silently compelled her—like that day in the shop, although she hadn't realized the connection as yet.

An entire week passed and Annie was able to get no closer to her crystal...but the same could not be said for Callum.

Despite his warning that he would "take her head," he treated her like a guest of honor, seating her beside him at supper, after they finally had a proper table built inside the great hall. She slept in his chamber "for her protection," he said. But Annie knew better. The bond between them grew stronger while her desire to return home grew weaker. She couldn't help herself. He drew her as inexorably as her Winter Stone.

She made love to him every night, despite his reluctance after that first encounter in the caverns. Something she had said must have upset him, because he tried to keep his distance, but Annie persisted. If he regretted their lovemaking after that first time, she found a way to make it up to him...waking him with her mouth, loving him with her body. She took him into her hands, worshipping him with her mouth and tongue. If he doubted her, all he needed to do was feel the emotion in every kiss she gave him.

She didn't understand any more than he did why that crystal and room had gone black. She hadn't lied to him. And it wasn't because she didn't want him. To the contrary, she wanted him enough that even the thought of conceiving their child didn't stop her. In fact, she couldn't imagine any greater bliss than carrying his baby home with her. She knew it couldn't stop her from leaving. She had her own destiny to fulfill, and maybe, if she was very, very lucky, she could take a piece of him home with her to cherish.

For Callum's part, he showered her with small gifts —things he fashioned with his own two hands—for one, a brooch carved out of ash wood that bore the symbol of his house. He made it to keep his cloak fastened tightly around her shoulders—to cover the plummeting neckline of Kate's blouse. Many of his kinswomen were dressed in far less, so she suspected it was his way of controlling his own temptation, and that knowledge pleased her. For once in her life, it felt good to be a bit of a temptress, and she had a sense for why Kate so often wielded her own sexuality like these men did their swords. This was the first time in Annie's life she had ever cared about such a thing, and it was as though he spoke to some primal instinct in her. Even so, just when he could have had any time to create the brooch when he was supervising just about everything else in this valley, she had no clue. But there it was. Beautiful, delicate and probably the finest gift Annie had ever received.

She watched the moon anxiously: It was waning, not waxing.

By the end of the week, she looked much more like the other women of Callum's clan. Dressed in her skirt, her untucked white blouse, she wore Callum's cloak instead of her cheap poncho, clasped by his brooch at her throat. She was thinking less and less of the Winter Stone and more and more of what it might be like to spend her life with a man like Callum. There was something quite satisfying to waking up in his arms and seeing him go to work and return to her each and every night. There was no wondering about his intentions, no niggling suspicions about late nights at work, or sultry meetings of eyes that made her question his loyalties. He made himself clear in every aspect of his life. Annie was not to be disrespected, he'd demanded of his clansmen, and no one dared defy him—and his seductive looks were all for her and no one else.

In the room they shared, she kept all her gifts from him in a single place, as though to keep them together so she could quickly pack them—as though she could take anything once she left this place. The truth was that Annie had arrived with nothing except what was on her person, the crystal included—and she suspected she could take nothing back. Absently, she touched her flat belly, and caught herself in the act, shocked by the wistful gesture. But she shook her head, forcing her thoughts back to the crystal. Somehow, she had managed to hold onto it during her nap—if in fact it had been a nap, because she still wasn't entirely convinced she wasn't dead and this wasn't truly heaven.

Because it felt like heaven.

Literally everything she had ever envisioned for herself was right here. She was surrounded by history, showered with the attentions of a truly good man. The more she learned about Callum, the more she liked everything about him. He was a man of strong principle, great kindness and loyalty to his people. He wanted to do the right thing by them all, and it was clear in every aspect of every decision he made—including his willingness to allow Biera to name his father's successor.

Annie might have been a little worried about her own pending trial, but by everything she saw from these people, they held Callum in great esteem.

Brude, on the other hand, was crude and overbearing and didn't inspire the same respect. But at least he had softened a bit toward Annie as well.

Callum walked in on her one morning while she was staring at the brooch he'd made her. "What are ye doing, lass?"

"Thinking..."

He sauntered in, and Annie stood to face him, feeling awkward. More often than not, lately she found herself staring at her boots, because every time she looked at Callum, she worried about leaving.

"Ye think too much," he said.

Annie's chest constricted as he stepped toward her, reaching out to gently take her chin. "If ye're worrying over Biera's return, dinna. I swore I'd let naught befall ye and I meant it, *mo chroí."My heart.*

Annie's heart squeezed. She nodded, and he bent to kiss her tenderly. And then without another word, he lifted her into his arms and carried her to his pallet.

CHAPTER TWELVE

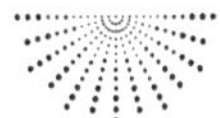

Callum worried about Annie.

After their encounter in the cave when her Winter Stone had grown cold, darkening the grotto, doubts began to plague him.

She had lied to him...but about what?

Over and over, he considered each word they had spoken. There had been nothing she had said that would reveal any answers. Nothing he could point to that might give away her intentions…unless, the stone did not need words—which made sense to Callum, for what use could a stone have for words? Mayhap her intentions had changed while in that grotto? Mayhap the stone had sensed something words could not conceive?

Biera had told him once that all things were born of love or fear.

Truth and lies, Annie had said—the Winter Stone could sense these things and by them foretell the destinies of men. But a lie could be told for the good of all, and a truth might be an evil thing. Mayhap truth and lies were simply words that did not tell the entire story? Mayhap her stone sensed paths that were either true or false? Decisions that were good and bad?

As he worked alongside his clansmen, he tried to

recall each of their conversations...searching for clues while he watched her slip up the hillside yet again, toward the rocky terrain that blanketed the area around the caverns. She ventured there nearly every day, seeking something.

But what?

Dunneld was shadowing her. If she attempted to leave the vale, Callum would hear of it at once, but she never seemed to try. Each day she returned to his arms and loved him as though she never meant to leave...

Or mayhap as though each time would be their last?

Callum had made a promise to her, and he meant to keep it...so long as she didn't betray him. Biera would return soon enough, and he knew the old priestess well enough to know that she would look for the good in Annie, though if Annie attempted to flee before Biera returned, there would be naught Callum could do to convince the rest of the clan that she meant them no harm.

There wasn't much chance she could hie away with the Destiny Stone itself, but if she chose to leave and then lead Giric back to the vale, there was naught he could do to stop her, for that then must be their destiny, and it was his people's belief that all things must come to pass as they should.

Which was precisely why he had been against bringing the stone here in the first place. He'd damned his father for convincing him otherwise for if that death stone—that sacred relic of those Dalriada kings—was destined now to bring war to those whose blood was not pure enough to rule two nations as one, then perhaps as Kenneth MacAilpín had begun his reign, so too would he and all his heirs live and die.

But now...now Callum had begun to believe that he had been brought here to this vale for a reason. That reason was Annie Ross. She was his mate for life, he sensed, and he would wed her now if he could... without Biera's blessing, even. But alas, he must be certain of Annie's intentions...for the wellbeing of his people. Now that his Da was dead, if Biera declared it must be so, then his life would no longer be his own. All he could do was wait...and watch...and hope.

Avoiding her decision was not going to work, Annie realized. Simply by *not* deciding, she *was* deciding. Clearly, though time wasn't as linear as one might suppose, it didn't seem willing to stop altogether. Tonight she could see no moon in the night sky.

Her memory was a bit of a trap. Everything she had ever read was rattling around in there somewhere, and she searched the stores of her brain for info on the moon. She had read somewhere that it took about 27.3 days to orbit Earth, but the lunar phase cycle was about 29.5 days. She had no idea at what point in the cycle she'd come to be here, but she did know that in as little as twenty four hours, she could see the new moon pop up in the night sky—sometimes longer when there was pollution involved, but there was no pollution here. The sky was as clear as she had ever witnessed it, with a beauty that was unsurpassed. Her eye scanned the lower heavens, knowing that's where the moon would appear, rising parallel to the horizon. So this was it. She calculated she had about twenty-four hours left—maybe thirty-six if she was very lucky.

After searching the entire area around the caverns, she knew there was no way inside, except through the cave entrance, where at least two men guarded it at all times.

She needed a distraction.

She had been watching the men work, and she had

an idea though she hated to do it—really hated to do it. But she had to create a big enough distraction that everyone would rush to see it at once—including the men up on the hill—*especially* the men on the hill. And she thought she knew how…and if it worked, she would be on her way home soon. Why that thought made her feel so glum, she suspected she knew, but she couldn't allow it stop her.

CHAPTER THIRTEEN

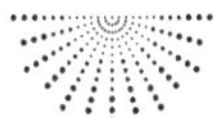

After a bit of a cold snap, the following day brought a bit of late summer warmth.

The sun shining down on the loch gave it a beautiful jewel-like appearance. Annie decided to freshen up. Keeping Dunneld at bay, she spent far too long swimming in the loch, and didn't come out until her fingers were pruned. But she was thankful for his show of trust. She shimmied back into her skirt, smiling over the reaction Callum had had to something so simple as a zipper. There was so much she had taken for granted...and hardly any of those things seemed important here. Televisions, who cared? All that was on anyway was news about war, politicians sleeping with porn stars and senators sending penis pictures to their interns. Here, there was the ring of children's laughter in the air, men shouted jests at each other over their labor, and the women worked side by side with the men. At night, they sat about the bonfire, telling stories, laughing and sharing whisky.

After nearly two weeks, everyone's hard work was coming together—buildings taking shape, and gardens being planned for the coming spring. A young lass by the name of Fiona showed her the seeds they would sow to plant their woad. Once harvested they would create their dye from it, as well as soap and a medicinal tincture.

In return, Annie gave Morag a tip about refrigeration. As she recalled, even the outer cave was freezing and filled with mist, especially where the cooler stream met warmer air. She explained the concept of refrigeration—obviously not in the context of electrical power, because that, she sensed, was more than these people could process. But she suggested they might want to use the cave to keep their cheese and other perishables stored. It was far colder in there than it was in a butcher's freezer. And the prospect of having old Morag's cheese stored for far longer than they were capable of doing now excited them. She was happy. At least she would have done *some* good here, considering the destruction she was about to create. All their hard work was about to come undone, but it couldn't be helped.

She had a very devious plan, and she had an unsuspecting helper in Dunneld, so she sent him to work, promising to give him her socks. He'd seemed enthralled by them as he watched her wash them in the loch. Of course, he accepted...because, indeed, winter was coming and thank God for one-size-fits-all.

CALLUM HAD a bad feeling settling in his bones.

He hadn't set eyes on Annie all day. Neither had he spied Dunneld's brilliant red head lumbering about. It was growing late now, and he was sweaty and tired and ready to sup and then to lock himself away with his wicked little faerie with the magic tongue and hands.

"Ha' ye seen Annie?" he asked Morag as he passed her near the pier.

"Storehouse," she grumbled, despite that she seemed

to have softened toward Annie since Annie had discovered a way to keep Morag's cheese fresh.

On the way he asked Brude.

His uncle stopped and scratched his head. "I saw her last going into the crannog," he swore. "Though I canna be certain. Ask Dunneld."

"I would if I knew where the bastard be," Callum muttered, more to himself. And then recalled that Dunneld had agreed to take the evening shift at the cavern's entrance this evening and he hoped to hell the man knew enough not to allow Annie into that grotto. She was a persistent little imp, and she knew precisely how to get her way. It had taken all his willpower to resist returning her crystal, for fear that it might be the only thing keeping her in the vale.

Mo chreach.

He craved the woman…like a drunkard craved whisky—which, by the by, he had a taste for at the instant and since he was near there already, he kept moving in the direction of the storehouse, fully intending to procure a dram and then to locate Annie.

Tonight he wanted to show her the sack he'd fashioned for her out of his share of the leather from their most recent hunt. She had been so disappointed by the disappearance of her dry blue sack, so he dyed this one blue, using the last of his woad paint. No more could be made until the spring, when the dye plants could be grown again and then picked. He'd pissed in the vat for three days in a row, until he was certain the stain was good and strong, and then he had immersed the leather sack into the dye bath and the color had set very well. The bright blue sack was drying now in the sun, and the thought of showing it to her pleased him immensely.

"Ach, Annie Ross, ye're my wee fae, indeed," he said to himself and shook his head, wondering if his Da was smiling in his grave at the thought of Callum's restless arse settling down at last with a bonny lass.

THE SETTING SUN brought back a chill. Out of nowhere, it seemed, a thin mist crept out over the hillside, peeking over the boulder where Annie lay hidden, waiting.

"Tonight?" the familiar voice asked.

Annie recognized it, though it wasn't until she peeked over the rock that she realized exactly who it was. Still, she blinked in shock. It was Dunneld—Dunneld with some other man. But she had distinctly heard them mention Callum by name and she was pretty certain she heard someone say something about *killing* him as well. Oh, no! She'd thought they were friends! And Dunneld had been so helpful earlier today when she'd had him move all the foodstuffs up here into the cave. She'd managed to convince him that it would be a safer place to keep their stores, and whatever perishables were in there would keep longer as well. The rest of the items had been easy enough for Annie to move herself. She'd put them somewhere where they might be found later after she was gone. Luckily, for the most part, everyone else had been distracted by the construction.

As she watched, Dunneld shook his head. "Why can we no' wait for Biera, Fergus?"

"The Crannog is nearly complete now. Once everyone is settled 'twill take the gods themselves to oust anyone from this god-forsaken place."

Dunneld tilted his head, as though pleading. "'Tis no' so bad here," he protested to the man he'd called Fergus. "Mayhap Finn was right? Mayhap this is the right thing to do?"

Annie thought he must be battling his conscience.

"Nay!" Fergus exploded. He was even bigger than Dunneld, with hair as fiery red as Kate's and a twisted bird painted on his arm and shoulder—one that looked a lot like the one on Dunneld's back. She thought she recalled this man from her first night in the vale, around the fire, but he must have remained in the shadows, never speaking. But then, of course, with Brude's drama that night, it would have been difficult to notice anyone else. His beard, like Brude's was forked and long, falling halfway to his fat belly. "Máel willna come here, and I willna force her," he said.

Dunneld's brow furrowed. "Ach, Da, but…seems to me you're putting your own good afore that o' the clan?"

Father and son?

"'Tis too late!" Fergus snapped. "Only the gods may intervene now!"

Annie's brain raced. *Too late? Too late for what?*

She was terrified for Callum. But there wasn't time to worry. Suddenly, she heard a terrible sound in the distance—a roar that sounded nothing at all like the explosion she had planned, but that's what it *must* be. It bounced off the hillside, echoing back and forth like rocks in a can.

Both men's heads turned in the direction of the loch. "What is that?" Dunneld inquired, frozen in a position to listen.

Fergus grinned and pulled at his beard. "That, my son, is the will of the gods."

CHAPTER FOURTEEN

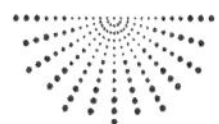

One entire side of the crannog came tumbling down, spilling into the loch with a crash that sprayed water halfway into the twilight sky.

At the monstrous sound, Callum froze on his way to the storehouse, realizing instinctively what it was. At the same instant, a second explosion echoed through the vale—this one coming from the direction of the storehouse. He turned in time to see flames shooting into the dusky sky. Within seconds, the entire building was ablaze and there was naught he could do to stop it.

Uncertain which way to go, he knew that the storehouse was lost already and that if any of his kinsmen had been caught anywhere near the crannog when it fell, they could be injured, or worse, dead. With nary a second to waste, he sprinted in the direction of the loch, and then a terrible thought occurred to him. What if, as Brude had said, Annie had gone inside?

When a second explosion came, Fergus and Dunneld peered at one another, and then, without another word both went racing down the hillside, leaving the cave unguarded.

Confused by the second explosion—this one sounding much more like a detonation of combustible liquids should—Annie sat frozen, uncertain what to do.

Her gaze sought the twilight sky, searching for any sign of the new moon. None was there to be found. And yet she knew instinctively it was time. *Now.* Tonight she *must* be standing up on that ridge in that field with her Winter Stone in hand—or else.

Or else what?

Or else she would be stuck here for all time.

She would never again see her cousin Kate again—nor any of her friends. Gone would be electricity and sushi and any chance of ever buying another awesome dry sack. Most importantly, the secret of the Stone of Destiny would be lost forever—or at least until another curious truth seeker came along. But it wouldn't be her.

Knowing it was now or never, Annie bolted up from her hiding place and raced inside. By the light of the pitch torches hanging on the cavern walls, she made her way quickly through the maze of caves and down into the lowest grotto, seizing her Winter Stone from where it had been placed on a ledge in the corner. And then as fast as her feet could take her, she made her way back out, adrenaline shooting through her veins at the realization that this was going to work after all.

In her hand, the stone remained dark for the first time since she had discovered it. Maybe its *battery* was shot, she thought wryly, as she rushed back through the caves, grateful for the pitch torches in their braces because the stone gave off no light.

Once outside, her feet took her automatically in the direction she knew she needed to go. Only then did the Winter Stone begin to glow…

THE LOCH CHURNED as bits of the crannog's roof slid into the water. Snapping under the pressure, another pile cracked, ditching more pinewood into the loch. Callum dove in, as immense logs continued to shoot like missiles into the water, not thinking of his own safety, only that of Annie's and his kin.

The chieftain's quarters were half submerged, and the roof was on fire, ignited by the burning pitch torches that were put in direct contact with the lowered thatch. Black smoke billowed into the bruised sky. Behind him, the burning storehouse sent more billows of smoke heavenward, and it seemed suddenly as though they had been sent to hell itself, for the skies turned ominous, and the waters of the loch blackened beneath a smoke-filled, moonless sky.

Once the churning waters stilled, he could hear the panicked voices of his kinsmen over the roar of flames. Those of his kinsmen who could swim continued to dive in around him, searching for poor souls who might have found themselves atop the structure when it collapsed.

By the sins of Sluag—it shouldn't have come crashing down. The building had been near to completion, and Callum had personally checked all the piles himself. They were new and sound, with solid, coated pinewood that should have lasted more than a few years.

Time after time Callum dove under the water to see what he could see, but the unsettled loch was murky and dark and the light was swiftly disappearing. His head came up suddenly, "Annie!" he shouted. "Annie Ross!"

Panic shot through him as silence replied.

Many of those who could not swim had congregated along the shore. Others ran from the loch with buckets to put out the storehouse flames. That fire burned bright and quick through the growing darkness, feeding on more than kindling. Purple and angry, the sky darkened the horizon and Callum scanned the banks to see who he could see.

Annie wasn't there.

His heart squeezed painfully in his chest. He didn't want to lose her—not this way. Not at all! She was the only reason he could remain here. Without her at his side, he had no will to stay. There were far better men than he to lead these people and the Destiny Stone would create its own fate, whether or not he remained in the vale.

"Annie!" he shouted again.

And then he heard her—the sound of her voice calling for him in the distance. He spun to see her racing down the hill—not her exactly, but her glowing orb. It burned like a God's eye in her hands. She ran toward him, shouting his name, and Callum swam back toward the shore with all his might, leaving his men to continue searching the area around the fallen crannog, drawn to Annie like a metal to a lodestone.

CHAPTER FIFTEEN

The damage was immeasurable.

Half the crannog had been destroyed, with many of the roof and floor joists having slid into the loch, unrecoverable. Most of the new thatch roof had burned away, leaving the interior exposed to the elements. More wood would have to be brought down from the forests, and with winter on the way, the work ahead of them would be long and arduous.

The storehouse was gone, burned to the ground, and it was fortuitous that its contents had been moved earlier in the day. Annie had apparently done that, though not alone, Callum was certain. She'd had an accomplice though she had yet to say his name.

The fire had been set apurpose, though far more grave was the fact that the piles on the crannog had been sabotaged. A few of the load-bearing columns had been cut below the water's surface. The rest had snapped and come tumbling down simply from the weight of it all. It was fortunate that most of the work for the day had been done, but two men and one woman had fallen into the loch, one of them dead now. Angus. Drowned, Callum may have surmised, except that his bloodless body was bloated. As far as Callum could tell, Angus had been dead for a day or more. There was foul play at work here. That much was certain.

They gathered now around *Clach Tolargg,* their meeting spot, to discuss the crimes committed. Everyone was present—no one excluded from these discussions. The decisions made here tonight would have far-reaching consequences, especially in regards to the stone.

"I *did* move the stores," Annie confessed. "And yes I *did* set a fuse to the kegs—I'm sorry." She shook her head. "But I had nothing to do with the crannog!" she denied the charge.

He'd allowed her keep to her Winter Stone apurpose. It glowed softly in her hands—a muted shade of pink. If he was right about the stone, he thought she must be telling the truth, though no one else seemed to see what he could see. They were calling for her head, and if he didn't find a way to prove what he suspected in his heart, she would die tonight by the blade. If it came to that, he would do it himself, for it only seemed right that it should be he who took her head.

The night was so black only the light from the fire and Annie's keek stane revealed aught. Emanating from her hands, it shone softly over her white tunic with the strange little clear knobs she had called buttons. His cloak was fastened about her neck with the brooch he had given her. And she was missing those strange garments she called socks. He noticed, however, that they were planted upon Dunneld's feet, looking a bit queer with his leather shoes. Callum didn't ask about that... not yet...he wanted to know something else.

He met Annie's liquid green gaze. He could see her clearly by the light of her orb even if no one else could. "Ye managed to get your Winter Stone...why di' ye not go?"

"It was dark," she said softly.

Callum tilted her a look, understanding what no one else could.

"That is…until I started running toward the loch," she said, looking him straight in the face, her lovely green eyes swimming with unshed tears. "Then it turned red, so I kept running," she said.

All sound seemed to fade away, save for the beating of Callum's own heart. Even the wind held sway. His heart squeezed. He peered around at his kinsmen. All of them appeared confused by her words…all except mayhap Dunneld, whose gaze was centered on Annie's socks on his feet.

A distant wolf's howl intruded, the sound doleful. That's how Annie felt right now. Her heart beat so loudly she wondered if everyone else could hear it as well, but she sensed that, like the glowing crystal in her hand, it was something only she could detect…along with Callum.

He sat upon his boulder as though it were a kingly chair, staring at her as though he were willing words into her mouth. She just didn't know what to say to make this right. She had done so much damage tonight, but the crannog wasn't her doing. That must have been the first roar she'd heard, and she suspected Dunneld and Fergus had had something to do with that, but if she spoke up now, and Dunneld was innocent, then he too would meet that shiny blade Callum had unsheathed and in his hand—a sword with an edge that gleamed greedily by the firelight.

She peered up into the night sky, spotting the new moon—just a tiny sliver in the sky—but the only true disappointment she felt right now was over the fact that she had let Callum down and betrayed his trust. The night was so dark that she could barely see his face, but she saw enough to note the dissatisfaction in his steely gaze. To say he was disappointed with her was probably an understatement.

She had saved everything inside that storehouse, except for the building itself and the whisky, but she didn't know what to say in her defense, so she said nothing. Seeing how hard these people worked, she realized it wasn't such a simple matter of going to the liquor store to buy more whisky or hiring men to put up a storage. She couldn't even hear anyone breathing. They were all waiting so still to see what Callum would say...what he would do...

"Ach! I leave ye fools but for a summer and what d' ye do?" a voice hailed from the shadows, shattering the silence.

Annie spun to see the whites of an eye and snowy hair emerging from the darkness, ambling toward the fire with a staff in her hand, a crystal similar to the Winter Stone its claw, glowing softly as she approached. Callum's kinsmen all parted to let the newcomer into the circle, and as she neared, Annie gasped in surprise.

It was the shopkeeper.

She turned to Annie first and smiled. "Ye did well, lass," she said.

"At last!" Callum exclaimed, rising from his boulder, and bringing his sword along with him. Annie winced and fell back a step, shifting so that she stood behind the shopkeeper, sensing the woman was someone important here. "Where ha' ye been, auld woman?"

"I said I would return afore the first snows fell and here I am," the woman contended, standing her ground as Callum came to stand before her. Annie hadn't noticed how tiny she was while in her shop—not until now when she confronted Callum. Inconceivably the little woman didn't seem the least bit afraid of him, despite that Annie wasn't feeling all that certain any longer, even despite all that had passed between them. The shopkeeper reached an arm out and pushed Annie behind her, as though to defend her.

"Ye know this woman?" Callum asked, but it wasn't a question. He seemed to sense their connection at once.

"I do," the shopkeeper confessed. "And well I should. 'Twas me who brought the lass to this vale."

Callum suddenly shook his fist at her. "At last! Something that makes sense," he declared, and he re-sheathed his sword.

The woman turned to Annie, bidding her to step forward, along with the crystal. "Ha' ye discovered the secret of the Winter Stone?" she asked, but Annie somehow knew she already knew the answer to that question. Her one-eyed gaze was entirely unnerving in its astuteness.

Annie shrugged uncertainly, but then she nodded, feeling maybe she did, in fact, know something she hadn't known yesterday.

The shopkeeper smiled. "They call me Biera, child, and ye're welcome for bringing ye home. Ye bear the Keeper's blood. Now come ye here and wield your stone and set the truth free at last."

Callum was looking at Annie in an all-new way. His gaze wasn't exactly filled with disappointment anymore. Maybe a bit of surprise.

Biera lifted a wiry brow. "Put your blade away, Callum mac Finn…at least for now." And she turned to look at Annie, giving her a nod.

Annie's heart gave a little nervous leap, but she tossed her cloak behind her and lifted up the crystal, looking straight into Callum's eyes. "I know who may have done it," she said, and turned and walked straight toward Dunneld, handing him her crystal. Surprised by the gesture, Dunneld accepted it, holding it nervously between them. Her yellow socks on his feet turned orange by its light. "I heard you talking to Fergus," she prompted, wanting him to confess on his own.

That's pretty much all it took. Still holding the stone, Dunneld stepped past her, toward Callum. "Ach, Callum! He said it was what needed to be done for the good of all," Dunneld announced to one and all.

"Lies!" Fergus shouted.

Dunneld continued, as though he had been holding it in for far too long. "I swear I didna know about the crannog!" In his hands, the Winter Stone's rosy glow remained strong. "I only agreed to help persuade the clan to go. I had naught to do with Finn's death!"

"Lies! Lies! All lies!" Fergus railed. "You are *no'* my son!"

Biera gave Annie a lift of her chin, and Annie rushed forward to seize the stone from Dunneld's hands. She marched over to Fergus and held it out to him. "Prove yourself," she challenged.

"I dinna want your bloody rock!" he screamed at her.

The sound of Callum's blade leaving his scabbard sent a shiver down Annie's spine. "Take the keek stane," he directed.

Behind Fergus, the clan gathered around, forming a circle, preventing Fergus's flight.

Annie's heart beat ferociously as she lifted up the Winter Stone once more, asking wordlessly for Fergus to take it.

Still he hesitated, his eyes meeting first Biera's and then scanning the rest of the clan. "What will this prove?" he asked, peering back at Callum. "It's just a rock!" And with that, he seized the crystal out of Annie's hands. The rosy color faded instantly at his touch and he threw it away.

Biera's voice rang out into the night. "One truth told with malice is more damning than a thousand lies!" she sang, her voice carrying through the vale. "Black is the color of fear, and fear is the absence of love and light! Fergus mac Aniel your fear has led you to malice against your own people!"

For a tense moment there was utter silence, and then Fergus said angrily. "Protecting the sons of those bastards is no' our job!" Now he spoke to the crowd at large, smacking his chest. "We are the sons of kings and this mad crone would have you hide your faces here in this vale! Your bones will rot here and your names be forgotten!"

Clearly tormented to have to speak against his own father, Dunneld spoke up again, his voice gruff with regret. "He convinced Angus to cut the piles and then he murdered him and put him in the loch."

"Bastard!" Fergus exclaimed. "Ye were never my true son! Ye're mother was a Sassenach and I knew ye to be a tailard!"

"Seize him!" Callum charged, his tone filled with fury.

Brude was the first to rush forward, seizing Fergus by the arms.

"And you!" Fergus spat at Brude. "You crave this fate no more than I do! Now your seed will wither in your cock and all your sons and daughters will be forgot!"

Brude yanked him violently by the arm, "I wadna kill a mon for my own design—much less my own brother, ye craven bastard! At least ye might ha' fought Finn like a mon!" Two more came forward to restrain him and together they dragged him away, shouting and spouting obscenities.

Stunned by the ordeal, Annie stood, watching them go, and then Callum was at her side.

"What will you do?" she asked him at once.

"Take his head," Callum told her, eyeing her neck pointedly. Annie shuddered and he added with a glimmer in his eyes, "Better him than you."

Biera came to stand beside them, and Callum turned to the priestess, his voice strained with emotion. "I would ha' believed this from your own lips if you had but told me, Biera. If you knew about Fergus, why di' ye no' speak to say so?"

The old woman gave him a sly smile and a lift of her white brow. "Ach, now, ye daft mon…ye know I didna bring the lass to tell ye any o' this. I only hoped she'd know what to do in my stead when came the time. And ye know in your heart why I brought her…an' I'll leave the two o' ye to glean the rest on yer own." With that, she walked away, snatching up the Winter Stone and turning toward them only long enough to give Annie a little wink. The crystal lit up Biera's hand, glowing green as she started up the hillside, toward the caverns —a spring in her step that seemed completely out of sorts with her advanced age. She held the Winter Stone up as she went. "Ye dinna need this to recognize truth," she imparted.

Callum reached out to curl his hand around the back of Annie's neck. "Ye had your stone and didna go," he said again. "Could it be ye mean to stay?"

Annie's smile returned. "Apparently."

"I love ye, Annie Ross," he said gently, and then heaved a sigh that made Annie feel loved in a way words alone could never have accomplished.

She knew in her heart this was the right thing to do. She'd felt it deep in her bones, and apparently her legs had known the right path even before her head had figured it out. The instant she'd even thought about Callum coming to harm, she had rushed to his aid. When you got right down to it there was nothing to get back to because home was in the arms of this man who loved her…the only man who had ever loved her, by the look of adoration in his eyes. She recognized it now that she saw it.

Up in the night sky, the new moon was like a heavenly smile, its slim crescent a lopsided grin—one that matched the silly one that lit Callum's face. "Will ye take me as your husband, Annie Ross?"

"I will," she said, and returned his embrace, wondering how much she should tell him about where she had come from, if anything. Maybe it was better if he believed she was a faerie, because if in fact his people were destined to vanish from history, then really all that was important was here and now…

"I have a gift for you?" he said.

"Another one?"

"Aye," he told her. "A blue sack. 'Tis dry now, at last, and 'twill serve ye well from sea to summit."

Annie smiled, remembering her first words to him, and then she lifted herself on tippy toes to kiss his lips, a gentle kiss that betrayed all the feeling that was in her heart.

"Now," he said. "About the whisky ye burned…"

"I'll learn how to make more," she promised.

"Aye, lass, ye will, on the morrow." And then he took her into his arms and kissed her more soundly, his lips claiming hers with ardor. Annie melted into his embrace.

Absurdly, she thought about Alice and Dorothy. Alice had found her way back through the rabbit hole and Dorothy had clicked her ruby heels. But Annie was perfectly content never going back, because Biera was right: *She was already home.*

GUARDIANS OF THE STONE

SERIES BIBLIOGRAPHY

If you loved the setting for Callum and Annie's story, and want to know what happens to the Stone from Scone, continue reading the legend with Highland Fire and Highland Steel ...

ALSO AVAILABLE AS AUDIOBOOKS

Once Upon a Highland Legend

Highland Fire

Highland Steel

Highland Storm

Maiden from the Mist

ALSO CONNECTED...

THE HIGHLAND BRIDES

The MacKinnon's Bride

Lyon's Gift

On Bended Knee

Lion Heart

Highland Song

MacKinnon's Hope

&

Angel of Fire

MAIDEN FROM THE MIST

Want to read more about Biera? Enjoy a brand-new legend. Sorcha dún Scoti has known her whole life she is different. Now, the future of her clan is in doubt, and Una, their beloved seer is gone. The youngest dún Scoti inherits Una's keek stane--and with it, the gift of sight. Here, the truth of her birth is revealed. Betrayed by her kinsmen and seeking answers, Sorcha must journey to a remote Island in the Outer Hebrides, where she hopes to reunite with Una. But despite her gift of sight, the truth holds perils Sorcha cannot foresee...

Stricken blind by his grief, Caden MacSwein has sequestered himself like a beast in his castle by the sea. It is whispered that he slew his own brother, and now is cursed by the Gods. When a maiden from Inverness arrives on his shores on the eve of the summer star, he soon sees with his heart what his eyes no longer will. But to restore his sight, Caden must ken his blindness comes from within... or he cannot save the maiden from the mist from the danger that pursues her.

Read Maiden from the Mist

GLOSSARY

Included here are just a few of the words and phrases I've used throughout my Scottish series. I often use learngaelic.net as a source, and just for fun, you might enjoy trying this Scottish translator: www.scotranslate.com.

Am Monadh Ruadh: the Cairngorms, literally the red hills distinguishing them from Am Monadh Liath, the grey hills

Aurochs: large wild cattle, now extinct

Bairn: baby

Bampot: idiot

Bean sìth: banshee:

Ben: mountain

Bliaut: men's and women's overgarment worn from the eleventh to the thirteenth century

Bhràthair: brother

bràthair-cèile: Brother-by-law

Breacan: short for breacan-an-feileadh, or great kilt

Bhrìghde: Sister of Cailleach Bheur

Bodachan Sabhaill: barn brownie

Brollachans: ghouls

Cailleach Bheur: the blue-faced mother of winter

Cairn: pile of stones, often built as a memorial or over a burial

Caoineag the Weeper: the banshee spirit who haunted the lochs and waterfalls. It was said she could be heard wailing before a death within a clan

Chreagach Mhor: great rocks

Clach-na-cinneamhain: stone of destiny

Claidheamh-mor: claymore

Clipe: a tell-tale

Corries: mountains, or hills

Crannóg: wooden dwellings the early Picts used as homes, often built over a body of water

Drogue: drug

Dwale: a drink made of nightshade or belladonna, often used for anesthesia

Fashious: troublesome

Gaol: jail

Geamhradh: Winter

Guarderobe/ garderobe: toilet

Keek stane: a scrying stone, or crystal ball

Ken: know

Leabhar: book

Loch: lake

Mac na h-Alba: son of Scotia

Minny: mother

Muckle: large

Pawky: having a sly sense of humor

Pechts: Picts

Quintain: a piece of training equipment used for jousting, often formed in the shape of a person

Reiver: raider on the English-Scottish border

Righ Art: the High King and Chief of Chiefs.

Sassenach: Englishman

Sùilean gorm: blue Eyes.

Scotia: Scotland, also known as Alba

Sìol Ailpín: the fractured Highland Clans who all claimed lineage to the first Ailpín king.

Tailard: an outsider, the enemy or an Englishman

Sluag: God of the Underworld

Siùrsach: whore

Targe: a circular shield used for defense

The Mounth: range of hills on the southern edge of Strathdee in northeast Scotland; bastardized version of Monadh. The mountain ranges are known as Monadh Liath and the Monadh Ruadh, which translated means Grey Mounth and the Red Mounth.

Trews: close-fitting tartan trousers

Uisge-beatha: whisky, literally means water of life

Vin aigre: vinegar or sour wine

Woad: a dye extracted from the woad plant

ALSO BY TANYA ANNE CROSBY

A brand-new series

Daughters of Avalon

The King's Favorite

A Winter's Rose

Rhiannon

The Highland Brides

The MacKinnon's Bride

Lyon's Gift

On Bended Knee

Lion Heart

Highland Song

MacKinnon's Hope

Guardians of the Stone

Once Upon a Highland Legend

Highland Fire

Highland Steel

Highland Storm

Maiden of the Mist

The Medievals Heroes

Once Upon a Kiss

Angel Of Fire

Viking's Prize

The Impostor Series

The Impostor's Kiss

The Impostor Prince

Redeemable Rogues

Happily Ever After

Perfect In My Sight

McKenzie's Bride

Kissed by a Rogue

Mischief & Mistletoe

A Perfectly Scandalous Proposal

Anthologies & Novellas

Lady's Man

Married at Midnight

The Winter Stone

Romantic Suspense

Speak No Evil

Tell No Lies

Leave No Trace

Mainstream Fiction

The Girl Who Stayed

The Things We Leave Behind

Redemption Song

Everyday Lies

ABOUT THE AUTHOR

Tanya Anne Crosby is the New York Times and USA Today bestselling author of thirty novels. She has been featured in magazines, such as People, Romantic Times and Publisher's Weekly, and her books have been translated into eight languages. Her first novel was published in 1992 by Avon Books, where Tanya was hailed as "one of Avon's fastest rising stars." Her fourth book was chosen to launch the company's Avon Romantic Treasure imprint.

Known for stories charged with emotion and humor and filled with flawed characters Tanya is an award-winning author, journalist, and editor, and her novels have garnered reader praise and glowing critical reviews.

Tanya and her writer husband split their time between Charleston, SC, where she was raised, and northern Michigan, where the couple make their home.

For more information
www.tanyaannecrosby.com
tanya@tanyaannecrosby.com

www.ingramcontent.com/pod-product-compliance
Lightning Source LLC
Chambersburg PA
CBHW070501170726
48291CB00008B/2598

9781947204188